The Case of the
Singing Skirt

Erle Stanley Gardner

BALLANTINE BOOKS • NEW YORK

Copyright © 1959 by Erle Stanley Gardner
Copyright renewed 1987 by Jean Bethell and Grace Naso

All rights reserved under International and Pan-American Copyright Conventions. Published in the United States of America by Ballantine Books, a division of Random House, Inc., New York, and simultaneously in Canada by Random House of Canada Limited, Toronto.

Library of Congress Catalog Card Number: 59-12866

ISBN 0-345-37149-6

This edition published by arrangement with William Morrow and Company, Inc.

Manufactured in the United States of America

First Ballantine Books Edition: June 1992
Second Printing: June 1993

Foreword

Gertrude Stein once sagely wrote "A rose is a rose is a rose."

To date no one has ever contradicted this statement.

In the field of legal medicine, however, when someone remarks "A coroner is a coroner is a coroner," there is an immediate chorus of discord.

Actually there are coroners and coroners and it is a far cry from the politically adept mortician in the small community who elects to run for the office of coroner and public administrator to my friend, Dr. Nicholas J. Chetta, the coroner of the Parish of Orleans, who has done such a splendid job of making New Orleans a bright spot in the field of legal medicine.

All of which goes to prove that no matter what title a man may be given, the sort of job he does depends upon his vision, his determination and his capabilities.

Dr. Chetta realizes that the ultimate function of the autopsy is to protect the living. The cause of death in any obscure case may be of the greatest importance not only to surviving relatives but to society.

In New Orleans, due to the fact that Coroner Chetta is ex-officio city physician, he has been able to bring about reforms that have helped legitimate law enforcement and have checked abuses in the field.

For instance, Dr. Chetta has placed a resident doctor on duty at the central police lock-up to examine all persons arrested, establish drunkenness or sobriety when persons are arrested and to supervise the welfare of the jail inmates.

Under Dr. Chetta, the parish has modernized and revitalized the coroner's office. Duly accredited pathologists now perform autopsies, and necessary pathological techniques are used in order to bring the coroner's office up to date as an aid to law-enforcement agencies in determining causes of death.

A photography department has been installed which is equipped for both color and black-and-white slides as well as prints. Autopsy findings are expedited through adequate inquiry by a special investigator.

A coroner's commission composed of doctors, lawyers and medical-school representatives serves in an advisory capacity.

Those who have had experience with law enforcement know the importance of determining with speed and accuracy the real cause of death, and it is my hope that my many millions of readers will come to understand something of the importance of legal medicine. It has a day-to-day impact upon their lives, their safety and the safety of their loved ones.

And so it gives me pleasure to dedicate this book to
My friend,
NICHOLAS M. CHETTA, M.D.
Coroner and ex-officio physician
of the Parish of Orleans

ERLE STANLEY GARDNER

Chapter 1

George Anclitas looked at Ellen Robb with the shrewd appraisal of a cattle buyer inspecting a shipment of beef. "Black stockings," he said.

Ellen nodded.

"Long black stockings, way up," George said, making a gesture which included the hips.

"Leotards," Slim Marcus added parenthetically.

"I don't care what you call 'em," George said. "I want the black shiny ones that are tight and go way, way up."

"That's the stuff," Slim said. "Leotards."

"And the skirt," George went on, eying Ellen appraisingly, "about halfway down to the knees with a little bit of a white apron. You know, that thing about the size of a pocket handkerchief with a lot of lace on it that you tie on."

"Tonight's the night?" Slim asked.

"Tonight we take him," George said.

"All of it?"

"Why stop halfway?"

"Now, he likes you," George went on to Ellen. "He can't take his eyes off you when you're in your working clothes. Every time after you finish a number, grab the tray and come on in. Always walk on the side of the table where he can see you and keep his attention distracted, except when I give you the signal."

"Now, don't forget that signal," Slim said. "George takes his right hand and rubs it along his head, sort of smoothing back his hair."

George raised a well-manicured hand to black, wavy hair and illustrated the signal.

1

"Now, when you get that signal," Slim explained, "you come right over to the table, but come up behind him. Now, get this. If he's only got two pair or three of a kind, you say, 'You want a cigarette, Mr. Ellis?' Remember, whenever you say 'you,' that means three of a kind or less. Now, if you stand back and say impersonally, 'Cigars, cigarettes,' that means a full house, and if you say 'Cigars or cigarettes' twice, that means the full house is higher than jacks. If you just say it once, it means it's below jacks—three tens and a pair of something, or three nines and a pair of something."

"And," George went on, "if he's got better than a full house, if he's got a straight flush or four of a kind, you reverse the order and say—"

Ellen Robb spoke for the first time. "No," she said.

Both men looked up at her incredulously.

"I'm not going to do it, George. I'll sing and I'll show my legs but I'm not going to help you cheat Helman Ellis or anyone else."

"The hell you aren't!" George said. "Don't forget this is a job you've got here, sister. I'm running this joint. You do like I tell you. What's the matter? You falling for that guy?" Then after a moment he added, less roughly, "It's only if I give you the signal, Ellen. I don't think we'll have to do it. I think we've got this sucker staked out cold. But he likes you. He likes to look you over. That's one of the reasons he hangs around. We've been fattening him up, letting him lose a little, then letting him win a little, then letting him lose some more. We know just about how he plays. But there'll be a couple of other fellows in the game tonight and that may make it a little more difficult to size up his play."

"I'm not going to do it," Ellen Robb repeated.

"Well, I'll be damned!" Slim said.

George pushed back his chair and got to his feet, his features dark with rage. Then he took a deep breath and smiled. "All right, girlie," he said, "go get dressed. If you don't want to, you don't have to. Just go ahead with your singing.

Just forget all the signals. We'll play it straight across the table, right on the up and up, won't we, Slim?''

Slim seemed bewildered by this abrupt change of manner. ''Well,'' he said . . . ''yes, I guess so . . . sure, if that's the way you want it, George. We can take him.''

''Sure, we can,'' George said. ''Forget it, Ellen. Go get your things on. Remember, black stockings.''

Ellen Robb glided from the room. Slim Marcus watched her hips until the green curtains had settled into place behind her retreating figure.

''Nice scenery,'' George said. ''But it's strictly for customers. Sucker bait.''

''What the hell's the idea?'' Slim asked. ''I thought you were going to give her the works, tell her to follow orders or else.''

Anclitas shook his head. ''It would have been the or else,'' he said. ''That dame has a mind of her own.''

''So what?'' Marcus asked. ''Who's running the place?''

''We are,'' George said, ''but we tie the can to her, take five grand from Ellis tonight and then she'd go to Ellis' wife and tell *her* the game was rigged. You know what'll happen then.''

''Keep talking,'' Slim said.

''The minute she refused to ride along,'' George Anclitas explained, ''she was done as far as I'm concerned. But there's no reason to be rude about it. When I get rid of 'em I get rid of 'em *right*.''

''What you going to do?'' Slim asked.

''Frame her,'' George said, his face darkening. ''Frame her for stealing and kick her the hell out. Tell her if she ever shows her face in these parts again, she'll be thrown in the can. I'll give her enough money for a bus ticket to Arizona and tell her if she isn't out of the state within twenty-four hours, I'll prosecute.

''She knows too much now. We have to discredit her. Remember that other broad we framed? She's still in.''

''Think we can take him without signals?'' Slim asked.

"Sure we can take him," George said. "We've done it before, haven't we?"

Slim nodded.

"Well, then, quit worryin'."

"I ain't worryin'. I just want to be sure."

"In our game, that's worryin'," George said.

Chapter 2

Della Street, Perry Mason's confidential secretary, stood in the doorway between the lawyer's private office and the passage leading to the reception room. An amused smile tilted the corners of her mouth.

At length, Mason, sensing her immobility, looked up from the volume he was studying.

"You have always said," Della Street observed archly, "that you didn't like cases involving figures."

"And that's right," Mason observed emphatically. "I want cases involving drama, cases where there's a chance to study human emotions. I don't want to stand up at a blackboard in front of a jury and add and subtract, multiply and divide."

"We now have a case waiting in the outer office," Della Street said, "involving a figure, rather a fancy figure I might add."

Mason shook his head. "We're booked solid, Della. You know I don't like routine. I . . ." Something in her manner caused a delayed reaction in Mason's mind. "*What* did you say the case involved?"

"A fancy figure."

Mason pushed the book back. "Now, by any chance, young woman," he said sternly, "is this an animate figure?"

"Very animate," Della Street said.

Mason grinned. "You mean it undulates?"

"Well," she said thoughtfully, "it sways."

"Smoothly?"

"Seductively."

"The age?"

"Twenty-four, twenty-five, twenty-six."

"And the figure?"

"Superb."

"The name?"

"Ellen Robb, formerly a photographic model. Now a singer in a night club, doubling as a vendor of cigars and cigarettes."

"Show her in," Mason said.

"It will be some show," Della Street warned. "She's garbed."

"Most women are," Mason said and then added, "when they visit offices."

"This," Della Street said, "will be different."

Mason placed the fingers of his left hand on his right wrist, consulted his wrist watch. "Pulse a hundred and twenty-eight," he said. "Respiration rapid and shallow. How much more suspense, Della? Now that you've aroused my interest to this extent, what are we waiting for?"

"What was the pulse?" she asked.

"A hundred and twenty-eight."

"In exactly five seconds," Della Street said, "take it again, and if it hasn't reached a hundred and eighty, you can cut my salary."

She vanished momentarily, to return with Ellen Robb.

Mason glanced quizzically at the determined young woman, who was wearing a long, plaid coat.

"Miss Robb, Mr. Mason," Della Street said, and then to Ellen, "If you'll slip off your coat so Mr. Mason can see what you showed me, he will . . ."

Ellen Robb opened the coat. Della Street's hands at the collar of the coat pulled it back and slipped it off the girl's shoulders.

Ellen Robb stood gracefully and without the least self-consciousness. She was clad in a tight-fitting sweater, a skirt which terminated some six inches above the knees, and black leotards. A small diamond-shaped apron, about the size of a pocket handkerchief, adorned with a border of delicate lace, was tied around her waist.

Despite himself, Mason's eyes widened.

"Miss Robb," Della Street explained, "won a bathing-beauty contest which included a trip to Hollywood, a screen test and a certain amount of resulting publicity."

"The screen test?" Mason asked.

Ellen Robb smiled and said, "It was part of the publicity. I never heard anything from it again. I sometimes doubt if there was film in the camera."

"The trip to California?"

"That was real," she said. "I had to wait to travel when the plane had some extra seats. However, it was nice," and then she added, "while it lasted."

"When did it quit lasting?"

"About six months ago."

"And you've been doing?"

"Various things."

"The last," Della Street said, "was being employed as a cigarette girl and novelty singer at a place in Rowena."

"Rowena," Mason said frowning, "that's the small town where—"

"Where gambling which doesn't conflict with the state law is authorized by city ordinance," Della Street said. "The place is just big enough to get incorporated. It pays its municipal expenses from the gambling and nicking the unwary tourist who goes through the eighteen blocks of restricted speed limit faster than the law allows."

"The police force," Ellen Robb said with a smile, "consists of one man. When he's at the east end of town, he makes it a rule to issue at least one citation on his westbound trip. People who are going east are immune if they go tearing on through. On the other hand, when the city's police force is at the west end of town, people going east had better crawl along at a snail's pace or they'll have a citation."

"I take it the officer is exceedingly impartial," Mason said.

"Completely impartial. He only gets one driver on every eastbound trip, one driver on every westbound trip. In an eighteen-block restricted district there's not room for a much better average than that.''

"I see you have a sense of humor," Mason said, "and now that Della has arranged the dramatic presentation of the principal figure in the case, why not sit down and tell me what's bothering you?''

Ellen Robb walked easily across the office, settled herself in the big leather chair, crossed her long legs and smiled at Perry Mason. "After all," she said, "I'm accustomed to being on display. I've had people looking me over so much I feel I could take a bath in a goldfish bowl at the corner of Seventh and Broadway without the least trace of self-consciousness—but that doesn't prevent me from being good and mad, Mr. Mason.''

"And what are you good and mad about?" the lawyer asked.

She said, "Five months ago I got a job with George Anclitas. He's running a place in Rowena, a little night club with a room in back where there are legalized games.''

"And your employment terminated when?''

"Last night, and very abruptly.''

"What happened?''

"George and his right-hand man and crony, Slim Marcus, were—''

"Slim?" Mason asked.

"His name is Wilton Winslow Marcus, but everyone calls him Slim.''

"Go ahead," Mason said, noticing that Della Street was making notes of the names.

"They wanted me to do some crooked work. They wanted me to look at the hands of a sucker and signal what he was holding.''

"And you did?''

"I did not.''

"So what happened?''

"I should have known better," she said. "George is dangerous. He has a terrific temper and he was furious. Then all

8

of a sudden he took a long breath and smiled that oily, suave smile of his, and told me it was all right, that he'd handle the game without my help."

"And he did?"

"I don't know. I didn't last long enough to find out."

"What happened—to you, I mean?" Mason asked.

"George told me the cashier had become ill and had to leave. I was to take over the cash register and let some of my singing numbers go. Well, there was a hundred-and-twenty-dollar shortage."

"While you were in charge?"

"Yes."

"A real shortage or—"

"A real shortage. The cash simply didn't balance."

"What happened to it?"

"Frankly, I don't know, Mr. Mason. I think George did a little sleight of hand on me when he inventoried the cash with me at the time I took over. George is very swift and very clever with his hands. He can deal from the bottom of the deck or deal seconds, and it's almost impossible to catch him at it. I think that when he counted the cash in the cash register with me at the time I took over, he used his sleight of hand. All I know is that when I came to balance up, there was a shortage of a hundred and twenty dollars."

"Who found it?"

"I found it."

"And what did you do?"

"I communicated immediately with him. I told him about it; that is, I told one of the waitresses to tell him. He was in this game."

"And what happened?"

"He fired me. I had about a hundred dollars coming in back wages. He handed me forty dollars and told me that was enough to get out of town on and if I wasn't across the state line within twenty-four hours, he'd have a warrant issued for me. He called me a thief and every-thing else in the—"

"Anyone present?" Mason asked.

"Quite a few people in the place could hear him," she said. "He wasn't particularly quiet about it."

"Know any of their names?"

"A couple. Sadie Bradford was there."

"Who is she?"

"One of the girls who does all-around work. Sometimes she acts as attendant in the powder room, sometimes she's a hat-check girl, sometimes she works in the motel office."

"There's a motel?" Mason asked.

"Yes. George and Slim own two whole city blocks. They have a motel with a swimming pool, a trout pool, a night club and bar, and a sort of casino.

"Some of the construction is modern, some of it is rambling old-fashioned buildings. The night club, for instance, started out as an old barn. George modernized it, put on an addition, kept the barnlike atmosphere and called the place 'The Big Barn.' "

"This Sadie Bradford," Mason said, "heard him call you a thief?"

"Yes."

"Would she be a witness?"

"I don't know. Her bread and butter might be at stake."

"What happened after he called you a thief and told you to get out of the state?" Mason asked.

"I wanted to go to my locker to get my street clothes, and he told me whatever was in the locker might be evidence, that he thought I had money secreted there. He handed me my coat and told me to get started."

"A rather spectacular way of discharging help," Mason said.

"He did it," she said, "for a purpose."

"To get even with you?"

"That was only part of it. They'd been playing poker for the last few weeks with this man, Helly Ellis—his first name is Helman—Helly is his nickname."

10

"And I take it this Helman Ellis was the man they wanted you to signal about."

"That's right. Last night they were ready to really take him to the cleaners and, of course, George was afraid that if I told what he had asked me to do, it might make trouble—so he chose this method of getting me discredited, firing me under a cloud, giving me just enough money to get out of town. He said he'd have my things packed up, put in a suitcase and sent to me at the Greyhound Bus Depot at Phoenix, Arizona. They'd be there in my name. I could call for them there."

"And when he cleans out your locker?" Mason asked.

She met his eyes steadily. "You don't know George," she said. "I do. When he cleans out my locker, he'll have some witnesses with him and they'll find a wad of bills."

"This was the first time you'd ever been in charge of the cash register?"

"No, I'd had charge before."

"Were there other shortages?"

"I think there were," she said, "but not in the cash register. I had heard George complaining that some nights the receipts dropped way down although business was good. He intimated that someone had been knocking down—only ringing up a part of the sales. He threatened to get private detectives on the job and said everybody was going to have to take a lie-detector test."

"I take it he hasn't won any popularity contests with the help," Mason said.

"Not recently," Ellen Robb said dryly.

"And somebody has been knocking down on him?" Mason asked.

"He seems to think so, and I would assume he probably is right."

"Could that person or those persons have tampered with your cash register?"

She shook her head. "Most of the knocking down that is done," she said, "is done at the bar. People who buy

11

drinks at the bar pay cash, and if the bar is very busy and the bartender takes in four or five payments at once, he can ring up varying amounts in the cash register and there is no one to check on him. For instance, let us suppose one man has a cocktail which is seventy-five cents or a dollar. Another man has a drink which is sixty cents. Another person has bought drinks for three or four, and his bill is two dollars and eighty-five cents.

"By timing things just right a good bartender can be preoccupied at just the right moment so that every glass gets empty at about the same time. That makes for a rush of business and a lot of payments being made all at once.

"So then the bartender picks up all the money, goes over to the cash register and starts ringing up sales of varying amounts.

"If the bartender is good at mental arithmetic, he can add up the figures in his mind and ring up an amount that is exactly two dollars short of the real amount. Then he gives each customer his exact change. Various amounts have been leaping into sight on the cash register, staying there for just a moment only to be superseded by another amount. Nobody can tell for certain what check is being rung up. If the bartender sees someone paying attention to the cash register, he is scrupulously accurate in ringing up the amounts, but if people are talking and not paying too much attention, he'll knock down a couple of dollars and no one is any the wiser. He'll do that perhaps ten to twenty times in an evening."

"Were you doing any of this work at the bar?"

"Not last night. I was handling the main cash register. I had the only key to it while I was on duty—at least, it was supposed to be the only key. I would sit there on the stool, and people would come to me with their checks, or the waitresses would come to check out the amounts due at their tables. I'd take in the money and give out the change."

"Was there any reason why you couldn't have knocked down if you had wanted to?" Mason asked.

"There's more of a check on the main cash register. The waitresses issue dinner checks and keep a carbon copy which has to be filed when they go off shift. Theoretically the cash register should show a total income equal to the exact total amount of checks issued by the waitresses. But there are lots of ways of beating that game."

"How?" Mason asked.

"Walks, for one."

"Walks?" Mason asked.

"A customer pays his bill directly at the cash register," she said. "The amount of the bill is two dollars and eighty-five cents. He gives you a twenty-dollar bill. You pretend to be very much interested in the addition on the check, then apparently something goes wrong with the key on the cash register. You concentrate on that. Eventually you ring up two dollars and eighty-five cents; still without apparently paying too much attention to him, you hand him fifteen cents, then give him two one-dollar bills, then hand him a five, then look back at the cash register for a minute. Nine times out of ten the man will pocket the change and walk away. If he starts to pocket the change and then stops suddenly, or if he still waits there, you take out two additional fives and give it to him with a smile, then start looking back at the cash register again."

"You seem to know all the tricks," Mason said thoughtfully.

"I've heard *some* of them," she said.

"And you sing?"

"Yes."

"Let's hear," Mason said.

She tilted back her head, sang a few bars of a popular song, then stopped and said, "My throat's always a little thick in the morning—I love to sing—I like melody, always have, but singing in rooms filled with stale tobacco smoke is hard on the throat."

Mason nodded, studied the young woman's face.

"You've had ups and downs?" he asked.

"Mostly downs," she said, "but I'm in there fighting. I think I'll go back to modeling. I can get by doing that— only there's no future in it."

"How does George Anclitas stand in Rowena?" Mason asked.

"It depends on whom you ask. He owns the justice of the peace and he has something on Miles Overton, the chief of police. As far as official circles are concerned, George stands ace high. Some of the citizens don't like him but they all kowtow to him. He's powerful."

"I think," Mason said, "we're going to interrupt a somewhat busy day to call on George Anclitas. You don't happen to know his telephone number, do you?"

"Rowena 6-9481."

Mason nodded to Della Street. "Get George on the phone, Della. Let's see what he has to say."

A few moments later Della Street, who had been busy at the dial of the telephone, nodded to Perry Mason.

Mason picked up the receiver. "George Anclitas?" he asked.

"Sure," the voice at the other end of the line said. "Who are you? What do you want?"

"I'm Perry Mason. I'm a lawyer."

"All right. What does a lawyer want with George?"

"I want to talk with you."

"What about?"

"About an employee."

"Who?"

"Ellen Robb, a singer."

"That tramp. What about her?"

"I'm coming out to see you," Mason said. "It will take me about half an hour to get there. Miss Robb will be with me. I want all of her personal possessions, I want all of the money that she has coming to her, and I'll talk with you about the rest of it."

14

"All right," George said. "Now I'll tell you something. You bring Ellen Robb out here, and she gets arrested quick. If she wants to spend the next sixty days in the clink, this is the place for her. Tell her I've got the reception committee all ready."

"Very well," Mason said, "and since you're planning a reception committee, you might go to the bank and draw out ten thousand dollars."

"Ten thousand dollars! What are you talking about?"

"I am about to file suit on her behalf for defamation of character, for slanderous remarks and false accusation. If you have ten thousand dollars available in cash, I might advise Miss Robb to make a cash settlement rather than go to court."

"What the hell you talking about?" Anclitas shouted into the telephone.

"About the business I have with you," Mason said, and hung up.

The lawyer looked across the desk at Ellen Robb's startled eyes. "Want to put on your coat and go?" he asked.

She took a deep breath. "No one has ever talked to George Anclitas like that. I want very much to put on my coat and go."

Mason nodded to Della Street. "Bring a notebook, Della."

Chapter 3

The Big Barn in Rowena was a two-story frame building, the front of which had been made to resemble the entrance to a barn. Double barn doors were half open. A recessed partition in the back of the doors, which was not over two feet deep but to which the ends of bales of straw had been fastened, created the impression of a huge barn crammed with baled hay.

A motel was operated in connection with the other activities, and a sign at the road blazoned TROUT FISHING POOL. RODS, REELS RENTED. FISH BAIT SOLD. NO LICENSE NECESSARY.

Perry Mason parked his car, assisted Della Street and Ellen Robb to the curb, then walked across to open the door to the night club.

After the bright sunlight of the sidewalks, the interior seemed to be encased in thick gloom. Figures moved around in the shadows.

A man's voice said, "I'm Miles Overton, the chief of police of Rowena. What are you folks doing here?"

Ellen Robb gave a little gasp.

"Where's George Anclitas?" Mason asked.

"Here I am."

George Anclitas pushed his way belligerently forward, his deep-set eyes glittering with hostility at Perry Mason.

Mason's eyes rapidly adjusted themselves to the dim light.

"I'm Perry Mason. I'm an attorney," he said. "I'm representing Ellen Robb. You threw her out of here last night without giving her a chance to get her things. The first thing we want is to get to her locker and get her belongings."

16

"All right, all right," George said. "You want to go to the locker. The chief of police is here. He'll search the locker."

"Not without a warrant he won't."

"That's what you think," the chief said. "When she opens that door I take a look. George Anclitas owns this place. He's given me permission to search any part of it I want."

"The locker is the property of my client," Mason said.

"She got a deed to it?" George asked.

"It was designated as a place where she could store her things," Mason said.

"While she was working here. She isn't working here any more. I want to take a look in there. I want to see what's in there. I'll bet you I'll find some of the money that's been missing from the cash register."

"You mean," Mason said, "that she would have taken the money from the cash register last night, then gone to her locker, unlocked the locker, opened the door, put the money in there, then closed and locked the door again?"

"Where else would she have put it?" George asked.

Mason regarded his client with twinkling eyes. "There," he said, "you have a point."

"You're damned right I got a point," George said.

"And you don't have a key to the locker?" Mason asked.

"Why should I have a key?"

"I thought perhaps you might have a master key that would open all of the lockers."

"Well, think again."

"You can't get in this locker?"

"Of course not. I gave her the key. She's got it in her purse, that little purse she keeps down in the front of her sweater. I saw her put it there."

"And you have been unable to open her locker?" Mason asked.

"Of course. Sure, that's right. How *could* I get in? She's got the key."

"Then," Mason said, "how did you expect to get her things out and send them by bus to Phoenix, Arizona?"

George hesitated only a moment, then said, "I was going to get a locksmith."

The police chief said, "Don't talk with him, George. He's just trying to get admissions from you."

"First," Mason said, "I'm going to get my client's things. I'm warning you that any attempt to search her things without a warrant will be considered an illegal invasion of my client's rights. I'm also demanding an apology from Mr. Anclitas because of remarks he has made suggesting that my client is less than honest. Such an apology will not be accepted as compensation by my client, but we are suggesting that it be made in order to mitigate damages."

George started to say something, but the chief of police said, "Take it easy, George. Where's Jebley?"

"That's what I want to know," Anclitas said angrily. "I told my attorney to be here. This tramp is going to show up with an attorney, I'm going to have an attorney. I—"

The door opened. For a moment the light from the sidewalk poured in, silhouetting a thick neck, a pair of football player's shoulders and a shock of curly hair. Then the door closed and the silhouette resolved itself into a man of around thirty-seven with dark-rimmed spectacles, a toothy grin and hard, appraising eyes.

"This," George Anclitas announced, "is Jebley Alton, the city attorney here at Rowena. The city attorney job isn't full time. He takes private clients. I'm one."

George turned to the attorney. "Jeb," he said, "this man is Mason. He says he's a lawyer and—"

Anclitas was interrupted by Alton's exclamation. "*Perry Mason!*" he exclaimed.

Mason nodded.

Alton's hand shot forward. "Well, my gosh," he said, "am I glad to meet you! I've seen you around the Hall of Justice a couple of times and I've followed some of your cases."

18

Alton's fingers closed around Mason's hand.

"All right, never mind the brotherly love stuff," George said. "This guy Mason is representing this woman who's trying to blackmail me and—"

"Easy, George, easy," Alton warned. "Take it easy, will you?"

"What do you mean, take it easy? I'm telling you."

Alton said, "This is Perry Mason, one of the most famous criminal lawyers in the country."

"So what?" Anclitas said. "He's representing a broad who's trying to blackmail me. She claims I accused her of being dishonest."

"Oh, George wouldn't have done that," Alton said, smiling at Mason. And then turning to Della Street, bowing, and swinging around to face Ellen Robb, "Well, well," he said, "it's the cigar and cigarette girl."

"That's the one," George said.

"What's the one?"

"The one who's making the trouble. Ellen Robb, here."

The chief of police said, "There's been a program of pilfering going on in the place. George has run up against a whole series of shortages. He's asked me to make an investigation."

Alton's eyes swept over the chief of police with skeptical appraisal. "The law of searches and seizures is rather technical, Chief," Alton said easily. "Several decisions of the Supreme Court in California and the Supreme Court of the United States haven't simplified matters any. I'll take charge here."

Mason turned to Ellen Robb. "Do you have a key to your locker?"

She nodded.

"Get it," Mason said.

Her hand moved into the front of her sweater, came out with a small coin purse. She opened it, took out a key.

"Let's go," Mason said.

Ellen Robb led the way. Mason and Della Street came

next, then the chief of police. George Anclitas, striding forward, was checked by Jebley Alton who, laying a restraining hand on his client's arm, drew him back to one side and engaged in rapid-fire, low-voiced conversation.

Ellen led the way into a room marked *Employees*, through a curtained doorway which had the word *Female* painted over the top, and paused before a locker.

"Open it," Mason said.

She fitted a key and opened the locker. In it there was a cheap suitcase, a pair of shoes, a suit and a raincoat.

"These all yours?" Mason asked.

She nodded.

"Do you want to put those things in that suitcase?"

"They came in that way. They can go out that way," she said.

"You have some other things?"

"Yes."

"Where?"

"There's a motel unit assigned to us girls. We sleep there. It's a sort of dormitory. Sadie Bradford, another girl and I share the unit. He wouldn't let me get my things out of it last night. I was virtually thrown out."

"Better start packing," Mason said.

She pulled out the suitcase and flung back the lid.

"I think Miss Robb would like some privacy while she changes her clothes," Mason said. "My secretary, Miss Street, will wait with her and—"

Mason broke off at the startled exclamation from Ellen Robb.

"What is it?" he asked.

She instinctively started to close the lid of the suitcase, then checked herself.

"Let's take a look," Mason said.

"I'll take a look," the chief of police said, pushing forward.

"What is it, Ellen?"

Ellen Robb reopened the lid, then pulled forward the elastic which held closed one of the compartments in the lining of the suitcase. A wad of currency had been thrust hurriedly into this compartment.

"I'll take that into my custody," the chief of police said.

Mason moved so that he interposed a shoulder between the officer and the suitcase. "We'll count it," he said.

Ellen Robb glanced at him in questioning panic, then with trembling fingers counted the money. "Five hundred and sixty-eight dollars," she said.

"Good," Mason told her. "We'll give George credit for that on the amount of back wages due and our claims against him for defamation of character."

George, who had quietly entered the room with Alton at his side, started to say something, but just then the curtained doorway was flung back with such violence cloth was almost ripped from the guide rings on the overhead pole. A woman's voice said angrily, "Defamation of character, indeed! *That's* a laugh—pot calling the kettle black, I'd say!"

Her eyes blazed hatred at Ellen, then she turned back to George.

"But I didn't come here to see that husband stealer, I came to see you. Just what do you think you're doing to my husband?"

"Why Mrs. Ellis!" George said, stepping forward and smiling cordially. "This is—that is—we aren't really open for business yet. I had some people come in and—Come on with me and I'll buy a drink."

She ignored the man's proffered hand, said furiously, "You've been trimming my husband in a crooked game here and I am tired of it. He tells me you took him for six thousand dollars last night. We don't have that kind of money to lose, and I'm not going to let you make a sucker out of my husband. I want the money back."

"You want it back!" George said incredulously.

"That's right, you heard me. I want it back."

George said soothingly, "Your husband was in a little private game last night, Mrs. Ellis. I don't know how he came out. I believe that perhaps he *did* lose a little, but I haven't tried to figure up just how much. I can assure you that the game was on the up and up. I was in it myself. If we gambled with people at night, let them take a chance on winning the place, and then, if they weren't lucky, gave them back the money they had lost the next morning, it wouldn't be very long before I'd be selling apples on the street corner."

He laughed at the idea, his mouth making the laughter, his eyes anxiously watching her, appraising her mood.

"As far as I'm concerned, that's exactly where you belong," Mrs. Ellis said. "I want our money back. That's money my husband earned, and I have other uses for it than giving it to you. I'm *not* going to let you cheap crooks rob us of that money and get away with it."

The chief of police said, "I hope I don't have to take you into custody for disturbing the peace, Mrs. Ellis. If you continue to make abusive statements of that sort in public, I'll have to take action."

"You!" she snapped at him. "You fatheaded nincompoop! You're just a shill for these gambling houses. George Anclitas has you right in his hip pocket. You don't dare to hiccup unless he gives you permission. Don't tell *me* what I can do and what I can't do!"

"You're using loud and profane language in a public place," the chief said.

"I haven't moved into profanity yet," she told him, "but I'm getting ready to, and when I do, I'm going to have some very biting adjectives and a few nouns that may startle you . . . you—"

"Just a minute," Mason interrupted. "Perhaps *I* can be of some help here."

"And who are you?" Mrs. Ellis demanded, turning to regard Perry Mason belligerently. "You . . . I've seen your pictures . . . why, you're Perry Mason!"

Mason bowed, said, "I think it might be better to control your temper, Mrs. Ellis. Apparently you aren't going to get anywhere making a personal demand, and I think perhaps a

22

written demand made in a more formal manner through an attorney would do you more good.''

"What are you talking about, through an attorney?" George said scornfully. "You know as well as I do that when a guy loses money gambling he can't get it back."

"Can't he?" Mason asked.

George laughed sardonically. "You're damned right he can't. Even if the game was crooked, he can't. He was engaging in an illegal activity and—"

"Careful," Jebley Alton interposed. "Let us put it this way, George. There are certain contracts that are against public policy as far as the law is concerned. It's against the policy of the law to raise those activities to the dignity of legitimate business enterprises. Therefore, the courts are not open to persons who have participated in those activities.''

"Never mind all that double talk," George said. "Let's give it to her straight from the shoulder. Tell her she can't get a dime back.''

"That's right, Mrs. Ellis," Alton said with his toothy smile. "You can readily understand how things are in that regard. A man can't sit in on a game at night, trying to win money, and then come back the next day and say that the activity was illegal and that he wants the money back that he's lost. If he could do that, he'd keep all of his winnings and then whenever he'd lost he'd recoup his losses. Now, George is in a legitimate business and—''

"And they've rigged up a deal on my husband," she said. "They had already got him for something over four thousand dollars. I was willing to let that ride. He promised me that he wouldn't do any more gambling, but they started in easy last night and lured him into the game. Then they started to take him. He thought his luck was bound to turn and stayed with it and—''

"And there you are," Alton said, shrugging his shoulders. "He was trying to win. If he *had* won, he'd have pocketed his winnings and both of you would have been very satisfied this morning. But he didn't win, so—''

"So I want my money back," she said. "The game was crooked."

"You can prove that?" George asked ominously.

"I don't need to prove it," she said. "*You* know it was crooked. Everybody here knows it was crooked. You aren't running this place on the square. Don't be silly."

"Those are words that would lay you wide open to a claim for damages," George said. "I suggest you be more careful, Mrs. Ellis."

"All right," she said, raising her voice. "All I know is that my husband has lost something like ten thousand dollars here within the last few weeks and I'm not going to stand by and see him robbed. Now, are you going to give him his money back or—"

"Definitely, absolutely, positively not!" George Anclitas interrupted firmly. "Your husband doesn't get back a nickel, and in view of what you've just said and the scene you've created here, he doesn't even get back inside this place. I'm leaving orders with the doorman not to admit him. If you'd come to me like a lady and told me that you didn't want your husband gambling here, he couldn't have got in last night. But you never said a word about it. He came and went just like any other man and he gambled. He's a good poker player. He knows what he's doing but he just happened to have a run of bad luck last night. That's all there was to it.

"However, now you've said you don't want him gambling here, that's good enough for me. We won't ever let him sit in another game."

Jebley Alton said, "I think that's fair enough, Mrs. Ellis. If you didn't want your husband gambling, I'm quite certain that George wouldn't have wanted him sitting in on the games. I don't think you ever said a word to George about not wanting Helly to gamble. After all, he's been trying his best to win. You don't have any legal recourse and—"

She whirled to Perry Mason. "Will *you* take my case against this crooked outfit?"

Mason smiled and shook his head. "That's not in my

line," he said, "and I'm pretty well tied up with cases right at the moment. However, I suggest you do get an attorney."

"What are you trying to tell her?" Jebley Alton asked scornfully. "You know that an attorney wouldn't do her any good. A man can't recover money he's lost in gambling. That's one of the most elemental features of the law."

"That's right, Jeb," George said. "Make this guy put up or shut up. It's easy for him to say a lawyer can get the money back, but he don't dare to back up his words. Now, go ahead and pin him down if he thinks he's so damned smart. Personally, I'd like to hear how some smart lawyer can get gambling losses refunded."

"Do you have a pen and notebook handy?" Mason asked Mrs. Ellis.

She looked puzzled for a moment, then said, "Yes, there's one in my purse."

"Take this down," Mason said. "You can tell your attorney about it, and you, Mr. Alton, might like to look up some law on the subject."

"I've looked it up," Alton said. "What kind of a runaround are you trying to give us? Ellis can't sit in a game trying to win and then come back and recover the money he lost."

Mason said, "Mrs. Ellis, if you'll just take down this citation to give to your attorney when you call on him, it may make a little difference.

"You see, Mrs. Ellis, there's a peculiar situation in the law of California. Ordinarily, gambling debts cannot be recovered, and since the gambling activity is against public policy, the courts leave the parties in the same status where they find them.

"However, as your attorney will tell you, in California, where we have community property—that is, property which is acquired *after* marriage as the result of the joint efforts of the husband and wife—the husband has the care and management of the community property. In business transactions it is presumed that his judgment is binding upon the wife.

25

But he does not have authority to give away the property of the community or to squander it without a consideration.

"So in a case where your husband lost community property gambling, *you* may well be able to recover it."

"What are you telling her?" Alton asked angrily.

"I'm telling her," Mason said, "to make a note of a most interesting case, the case of Novo versus Hotel Del Rio, decided May 4, 1956, and reported in 141 C.A. 2nd at page 304. It's in 295 Pac. 2nd 576. In that case it was held that a husband has no right to gamble with the community property. His action is not binding on the wife. She can follow the community funds and recover them from the gambler who won them."

"What the hell are you talking about?" Jebley Alton said. "A decision like that . . . why, that would put gambling out of business."

"I suggest you look up the decision," Mason said. "It's an interesting law point. It may well put certain types of gambling out of business."

"What were those figures again?" Mrs. Ellis asked.

"141 C.A. 2nd 304," Mason said, "295 Pac. 2nd 576. Ask your lawyer to look up the decision."

Mason turned to George Anclitas. "I'll be in touch with your attorney about Miss Robb's claim for damages on defamation of character and on being discharged without cause, on being thrown out with only the sheerest of garments to cover her body.

"And as far as you're concerned, Mrs. Ellis, I would suggest that you get an attorney, preferably someone who is not living in Rowena and dependent on the local political machine for any favors."

Mrs. Ellis said with feeling, "If that's the law, if wives can get back what their husbands lose in these joints, there's going to be a cleanup in Rowena. I know a dozen women who are fighting mad over the way this thing's been run and the way their bank accounts melt away only to reappear in the hands of these men who run dives of this sort."

"It's a thought," Mason said. "The situation has very great possibilities, and that decision of the court may have far-reaching repercussions. Perhaps your attorney would like to appear before one of the local women's clubs and give a talk on California law and the management of community property."

Mrs. Ellis said, "I'm tremendously indebted to you, Mr. Mason."

"Not at all," Mason said.

"This guy's nuts," George Anclitas said to Mrs. Ellis. "I don't know what his idea is in filling you up with this stuff but I know what the law is. I've been in the gambling business for a long time and . . ."

His voice trailed away into silence as he got a look at Jebley Alton's face.

"What the hell, Jeb!" he said. "You don't think there's anything to that cock-and-bull theory, do you? I know what the law is in regard to gambling."

Jebley Alton said thoughtfully, "Apparently this case was decided in regard to community property. It *may* be there's a quirk in the law that—I'll go up to the office and look up the decision."

"You do that," Mason said, smiling. "It is a very interesting case."

George turned to Mrs. Ellis. "Now, you look here, Mrs. Ellis," he said, "you and I aren't going to get at loggerheads with each other. My attorney's going to look up that decision. There's no need for *you* to go getting a lawyer and *you* don't need to bring anyone in to make any talk before any women's club. That stuff is for the birds."

Mrs. Ellis laughed throatily. "What a wonderful coincidence," she said. "It happens that I'm in charge of the entertainment program for the next three months at the Rowena Women's Club. We have a regular monthly meeting about ten days from now, and I was wracking my brains, trying to think of some really entertaining program that would be of universal interest.

"This is a program that will bring everyone out. There must be dozens of women here who will want to learn about the law of community property as it relates to gambling."

"And now," Mason said, bowing to George Anclitas and his openmouthed attorney, "I think we'll go out to the car, Della, and let our client finish dressing. She can pack her things and leave here at her convenience."

Mason turned to Ellen Robb. "I'm quite satisfied you won't have any more trouble, Miss Robb."

"What about this money?" she asked, pointing to the money in the suitcase.

"Remember the amount," Mason said. "Give George credit for that as payment on account. Go to a hotel, get a room, and let me know where you are."

"They'll arrest me the minute you leave here," she said.

"I don't think so," Mason replied, smiling. "I think they'll treat you with every consideration."

Mason turned so that the others could not see him and gently closed his right eye. "As it happens, Miss Robb, I am primarily interested in the better administration of justice and don't care particularly about fees. I hate to see people pushed around just because they don't have political influence. In case you want to make some settlement with George Anclitas on your own, it's quite all right with me. Just make any kind of a deal you think is fair and don't worry about my fee. There will be no charges.

"If, on the other hand, the slightest indignity is offered you or any threats are made, don't fail to call me at my office."

Jebley Alton said, "I don't know what you mean by a settlement. As far as Ellen Robb is concerned, she's getting out pretty easy if she keeps that money and—"

"You get the hell back up to your office," George Anclitas interrupted, "and look up that damned decision. If that thing says what Mason says it says, there are certain things we've got to do—fast."

"It is," Mason said, "a decision which presents an interesting problem to you people who are making a living out of gambling.''

Mason extended his arm to Della Street and together they left The Big Barn.

Mason held the car door open for Della, then walked around and got in behind the wheel.

The lawyer was chuckling as they drove out of Rowena.

"Chief," Della Street said in an awed tone, "does that case of Novo versus Hotel Del Rio lay down the law that you said it did?''

Mason smiled. "Look it up when you get back to the office, Della. The doctrine laid down may be limited in future cases, but in that case the court said very plainly that transfer by a husband of community funds in payment of a gambling debt was within the meaning of the law a transfer without the consent of the wife and without the receipt of any valuable consideration by the husband. It's quite a decision.

"I can imagine that when some attorney delivers a talk on the law of community property to the housewives of Rowena and reads this decision, the meeting will be very, very well attended.''

"And you deliberately walked off and left Ellen Robb there so that George could make a settlement with her?''

"I thought perhaps under the circumstances he *might* have a change of heart. You know, Della, I wouldn't be too surprised if he didn't also reach some sort of an understanding with Mrs. Ellis.

"I think on the whole it's been a rather unprofitable morning for George Anclitas.''

"Well," Della Street sighed, "you can't say he's the only one. We've lost half a day from the office, given some attorney a whole lot of fees on a silver platter, making him the fair-haired boy child for the women of Rowena. We've thrown any fee in the Robb case out of the window, in addition to gasoline and mileage on the car.''

"I know," Mason said, "but think of the enjoyable morning, the sunshine, the fresh air, the scenery."

"Particularly the scenery," Della Street said sweetly.

"Yes, indeed, the scenery," Mason agreed. "And somehow, Della, I have an idea we'll receive a phone call from Ellen Robb shortly after we get back to our office."

"Wanting to know about what to settle for?"

"Something like that," Mason said.

"What should she settle for?"

"About anything she can get," Mason said. "I think George Anclitas has learned his lesson. I think Ellen Robb has been fairly well compensated for whatever inconvenience was caused her by being thrown out clad in nothing much but a sweater and stockings."

"She doesn't mind that," Della Street said. "She's accustomed to appearing in public with nothing much on. She likes it."

"Tut, tut," Mason said, "don't sell our client short."

"If it had been a man," Della Street asked, "would you have done as much in the interests of justice?"

Mason thought for a moment, then met her eyes. "Hell no," he admitted.

"Leotards," Della said somewhat wistfully, "are hardly suited for office wear, but they certainly can do things for a girl."

"They certainly can," Mason agreed.

Chapter 4

Perry Mason latchkeyed the door of his private office.

Della Street, who had been sorting the mail, looked up with a smile.

"Well, Della," the lawyer said, "I wonder what adventures the day holds."

"Let us hope that it's nothing that will take your mind from the brief in the Rawson case or the stack of mail that I've marked urgent and have been calling to your attention for the last two days."

Mason settled himself in his swivel chair and sighed. "I presume one can't go through life just skimming the cream off existence," he said. "Sooner or later one has to get down to chores, routine drudgery. But I really did enjoy yesterday, Della. It was in the nature of an adventure.

"Now I'm somewhat in the position of the housewife who has given a very successful party, has ushered the guests out with cordial good nights and walks out into the kitchen to find a sink full of dirty dishes."

Mason sighed and picked up the folder Della Street had marked urgent. He opened it, hurriedly read through the letter that was on top, tossed it over to Della and said, "Write him that it will be impossible for me to be in San Francisco and take part in the case, Della."

Della Street raised her eyebrows slightly.

"I know," Mason said. "He makes a nice offer, but I don't want to try a case with him. He has the reputation of being a little too zealous on behalf of his clients, particularly in connection with producing witnesses who swear to alibis. What's the next one, Della?"

31

Della Street's telephone buzzed discreetly.

Della picked up the instrument, said, "Yes, Gertie," then looked at Mason and smiled. "A little more cream to be skimmed," she said. "Our friend, Ellen Robb, the singing skirt with the long legs, is in the reception room. She wants to know if it would be possible to see you. She says she'll wait the entire morning if you can give her just a few minutes. Gertie says she seems rather upset."

"Of course I'll see her," Mason said.

"Tell her to wait just a few minutes," Della Street told the receptionist, "and Mr. Mason will try to see her."

Mason pushed the file of urgent correspondence back.

"I thought we might have time for the other two letters that are on top. They're both urgent," Della Street said. And then added, "Miss Robb is probably conventionally dressed this time."

Mason grinned. "So the cream won't be as thick."

"Something like that," Della Street said. "Let us say that the scenic dividends may not be as great."

"You don't like her, do you, Della?"

"She has her points," Della Street said. "I should say her curves."

"And you don't approve?"

"There's something about her, Chief," Della Street said, "and frankly I don't know what it is."

"Something phony?"

"You have the feeling that she's . . . oh, I don't know. The girl's an exhibitionist. She's been capitalizing on a pair of wonderful legs and a beautiful figure. She uses them. Her singing voice is pleasing but it doesn't have much range. Her figure is her best bet."

"Pushing herself forward?" Mason asked.

"Oscillating is the word," Della Street said. "Of course, a woman with a figure like that, who is working in a place of that type is pretty apt to have been around, and . . . well, it would be interesting to know just what there is in her background, how she happened to be making her living that way."

"You mean she's probably done about everything?" Mason asked.

"Except teach Sunday school," Della Street said dryly.

"And you're warning me," Mason said, "not to become so fascinated by a pair of beautiful legs that I lose my perspective."

"Not only legs," Della Street said. "I have a feeling that she deliberately puts herself on exhibition in order to get what she wants."

"But this time," Mason said, "she will be conventionally garbed."

"She may be conventionally garbed," Della Street said, "but I'm willing to bet she's wearing something that's cut rather low in front and that, during the course of the conversation, she finds occasion to bend over your desk for some reason or other."

"It's a thought," Mason said. "Cough when she does it, will you?"

"Why?"

"So I can keep my perspective," Mason said, grinning. "Let's get her in, Della, and then we can get back to the routine of the urgent mail."

Della Street nodded, walked out to the outer office and a moment later came back with Ellen Robb.

Ellen Robb was wearing a skirt which was tight around the hips, with a band of pleats around the bottom which flared out as she swung around, displaying her knees. Her silk blouse revealed shapely curves. She wore a heavy pin at the closing of the low V-cut neckline.

"Oh, Mr. Mason," she said impulsively, "I feel like a heel coming in and taking up your time this way, but I desperately need your advice."

"About a settlement with George?" Mason asked.

She made a little gesture with her shoulders. "George is a lamb," she said. "He was as nice as I've ever seen him. He thanked me, Mr. Mason. He positively thanked me."

"For what?" Mason asked, indicating a chair.

33

Ellen Robb sat down and almost immediately crossed her knees. "Thanked me," she said, "for showing him what a heel he was. He told me that he was too accustomed to having his own way, that he was ruthless with other people and that it was a trait he was trying to overcome. He begged me not to leave him but to stay on, and he raised my wages twenty-five dollars."

"A week?" Mason asked.

"A week," she said.

"And you agreed to stay?"

"For the time being."

"So you're all straightened up with George?"

She nodded.

"Then what did you want to see me about?"

"The Ellis situation."

"What about it?"

"I'm afraid you started something with Mrs. Ellis."

"That was the general objective I had in mind," Mason said.

"Well, it goes a lot deeper than just a legal point, Mr. Mason. There's friction between Mr. Ellis and his wife. He thinks it would make him look like a piker for her to try and get back the money that he lost."

Mason said somewhat impatiently, "I tried to help you, Miss Robb, because I felt you had been wronged, but I can't adopt the troubles of the whole neighborhood."

Ellen Robb inched forward in the chair until she was sitting on the edge. She leaned forward to put her hands on the arm of Mason's chair. "*Please*, Mr. Mason," she said, "I didn't mean it *that* way."

Della Street coughed.

Mason looked at Ellen Robb, then glanced at Della Street. "Go ahead, Miss Robb," he said.

She said, "I'm so anxious that you understand, Mr. Mason, that I . . . I'm just coming to you because . . . well, because you do understand."

She sighed and straightened up once more in the chair,

34

glanced down at her knees, pulled the hem of the dress lightly with her thumb and forefinger and said, "Helly has gone overboard."

"Helly?" Mason asked.

"Helman Ellis, the husband."

"Oh, yes. And what's he done?"

She said, "Look, Mr. Mason, I'm under no illusions about myself. I'm on display. I'm sucker bait. I have a good figure and I know it, and I'm supposed to let other people know it. That's part of the job."

"And Helly, as you call him, has noticed it?" Mason asked.

"I'll say he's noticed it! He noticed it right from the start. Last night he— Mr. Mason, he asked me last night if I'd run away with him. He wanted to throw up the whole business and start all over again."

"What did you tell him?"

"I told him no."

"Well?" Mason asked, somewhat impatiently.

"All right," she said, "I'll get to the point. Nadine Ellis went to an attorney, a Mr. Gowrie. Do you know him?"

"Darwin Gowrie?" Mason asked.

"Darwin C. Gowrie," she said.

"I've heard of him," Mason said. "Quite a divorce lawyer, I believe."

"That's right. Mr. Gowrie called early this morning. He wanted to talk with me. He said he was Nadine's attorney— I thought, of course, it was about the legal point you had raised about the gambling, but I couldn't imagine why he wanted to talk with me. I thought he would want to talk with George."

"But you saw him?"

"I saw him," she said, "and it seems what he really wanted was to question me about Helly."

"Getting evidence for a divorce?"

"I don't know. He asked me all about my relationship with Helly, how long I'd known him, how many times he had

35

been at the club, whether he noticed me and . . . well, whether he'd ever made passes at me.''

"Had he?" Mason asked.

"Of course," she said.

"And you told this to Gowrie?"

"No."

"You lied?"

"I lied."

"Convincingly?" Mason asked.

"I hope so," she said. "Isn't a woman supposed to . . . well, isn't there supposed to be sort of a code of ethics about—?"

"Professional confidences?" Mason asked.

"Something like that."

"I wouldn't know," Mason said. "Why do you come to me?"

"Because I want your advice."

"On what point?"

"I want to go to Mrs. Ellis and tell her."

"Tell her what?"

"Tell her she is wrong about Helman and me and shouldn't make a fool of herself. She has a very fine husband. She'd better hang on to him. I've seen too many instances of women divorcing a man over some little thing and then regretting their action."

"Making passes is a little thing?" Mason asked.

"Of course. They all do—that is, nearly all—and I wouldn't give a snap of my finger for those who don't. Most of them don't really mean a thing by it. It's just the normal biological reaction of the male animal."

"You intend to explain that to Mrs. Ellis?"

"Not that so much as . . . well . . . the facts of marriage."

"What," Mason asked, "are the facts of marriage?"

"A man asks a woman to marry him because he enjoys her companionship. As long as he enjoys her companionship he's going to stay home with her. When he begins to wander

36

around, it's because something has happened to take the keen edge off that enjoyment.''

"Doesn't that happen with time?" Mason asked.

"It can," she said. "But the point is that when it does, the natural thing for the woman to do is to start reproaching the man, throwing it up to him that he's neglecting her, that he's getting tired of her now that she's given him the best years of her life, and all of that.''

"You seem to know a lot about it," Mason said.

"I've been through it," she said.

"And played your cards wrong?" Mason asked.

"Just as wrong as I could have played them," she said. "I lost a mighty good man. If I'd only had sense enough to make it a pleasure for him to come home, he'd have stayed home. Instead of that, I made the home a hell on earth for him and pushed him right into the arms of a cheap little tramp who took him to the cleaners.''

"But then he came back?" Mason asked.

She shook her head.

"Why not?"

"Let's not go into that," she said.

"All right," Mason told her. "What do you want to know?"

"Whether you think, under the circumstances, I should go to Mrs. Ellis and tell her exactly . . . well, put my cards on the table. I don't want her husband. I wouldn't have him on a bet. He's . . . well, he just doesn't appeal to me, that's all.''

"But you appeal to him?"

"Apparently," she said. And then added, "And to about ninety per cent of the other customers. Otherwise I wouldn't have lasted for the five months I've been there.

"I'm sorry for Helly. I've given him some sisterly advice. I'd like to talk to her. I—''

The phone rang.

Della Street answered it, then cupped her hand over the mouthpiece and said, "It's for you personally, Mr. Mason.''

Mason raised his eyebrows.

"Want to take it in the law library?"

"I'll take it here," Mason said. "Who is it?"

"An attorney," Della Street said.

Mason, suddenly warned by something in her manner, hesitated. "It is . . . ?"

She nodded.

Mason said, "Oh, well, I may as well take it here anyway. Let's find out what it is he wants."

Mason picked up his own phone, and Della Street threw a switch which connected both phones.

"Hello," Mason said.

"Perry Mason?" a man's voice asked.

"That's right."

"I'm Darwin C. Gowrie, Mr. Mason."

"Oh, yes, Mr. Gowrie."

"I'm calling you on behalf of Mrs. Helman Ellis—that is, it's in relation to a matter you discussed with Mrs. Ellis yesterday."

"What can I do for you?" Mason asked.

"That's a most interesting case you gave Mrs. Ellis yesterday," Gowrie said. "I feel rather guilty going before a women's club and stealing your thunder. Wouldn't you like to appear with me and take the credit for having ferreted out this decision?"

"Not me," Mason said. "If that's all that's worrying you, you have a complete clearance and a free hand. Go ahead and tell them about it. You don't need to mention my name."

"I've looked up the case," Gowrie said. "It's certainly a very interesting and yet a very logical application of the law. But do you realize what it's going to mean if this case is publicized? It's going to put the gamblers out of business. They just can't afford to buck a situation like that."

Mason said, "I spread it on a little thick for the benefit of George Anclitas. Actually it's an appellate decision. The State Supreme Court or the United States Supreme Court may not go that far."

38

"I understand," Gowrie said, "but right now that decision is on the law books in California. The gamblers are going to have quite a time over that. What do you suppose would be the effect if some married man went to Las Vegas and got in a really big game where he lost perhaps eighty or a hundred or a hundred and fifty thousand dollars of community property?"

Mason said rather impatiently, "I don't know. You can cross that bridge when you come to it. As a matter of fact, Gowrie, I have a file of a lot of unusual decisions, feeling that the time may come when I can use them. But I don't go out of my way looking for an opportunity to use them.

"Take, for instance, the case of a person shooting another person, inflicting a mortal wound, but before the wound actually proves fatal, while the victim is lying there mortally wounded, another person comes along and fires a second shot into the victim, and the victim dies as the result of that second shot—who's guilty of the murder?"

Gowrie thought for a minute, then said, "Both of them."

"That's wrong," Mason said. "There are quite a few well-reasoned decisions that hold to the contrary. There's a case in Arkansas—the case of Dempsey versus State, where one man stabbed a victim in the heart. Another man inflicted a fatal blow on the head. The last one was held to be guilty of the homicide."

"What!" Gowrie exclaimed incredulously.

"That's right," Mason said. "In fact, in California we have an early case holding somewhat the same thing."

Gowrie became very much excited. "Look, Mason, I don't want to poach on your private preserves—but now that you've given me the clue, I could pick up the citations at the law library. Would you mind giving me the citations, if you have them?"

Mason nodded to Della Street, said, "Just a minute, Gowrie."

Della Street opened a small card file, ran through the cards, picked out a card, handed it to Mason.

39

"Here are the citations," Mason said, "that I have on my card. Dempsey versus State, 83 Ark. 81; 102 S. W. 704; People versus Ah Fat, 48 Cal. 61; Duque versus State, 56 Tex. Cr. 214; 119 S.W. 687."

"Well, I'll be damned," Gowrie said. "You mean if I should shoot you and just as you were dying somebody else fired a shot that was instantly fatal, I wouldn't be guilty of any crime?"

"I didn't go so far as to say that," Mason said. "What I said was that you couldn't be convicted of murder—unless, of course, two people were acting together in accordance with a common plan, as the result of a conspiracy, or in the commission of a felony. In that event you would both be guilty of first-degree murder. But I think the law is quite plain that where a person has received a fatal injury but is not yet dead, and another entirely independent agency inflicts a wound which is immediately fatal, the second person is the one who is guilty of the homicide. However, I just mentioned that as an illustration. I have a whole drawer full of unusual decisions, and this gambling decision just happened to be one of them. You go ahead and use it any way you want to.

"Now, while we're on the subject, Gowrie, your client, Nadine Ellis, feels that Ellen Robb has been breaking up her home and—"

"Not at all, not at all," Gowrie interrupted. "I'm afraid Miss Robb had the wrong impression. I will admit that I was questioning her, trying to find out something about Helman Ellis and I'll also be perfectly frank to state that I don't know just what Mrs. Ellis is going to do about it. There's no question but that Ellis has been hanging around The Big Barn because he was interested in Ellen Robb. That's why they keep the girl there. They have her appear in clothes which show off her figure, and she has a figure that's worth showing off.

"Helman Ellis became completely fascinated. I'm not blaming the girl. I don't think she was guilty of any wrongdoing at all, but naturally, as Mrs. Ellis' attorney, I *would*

40

like to know a little of what was going on. You might tell your client, Mr. Mason, that I think she was a little less than frank with me. I don't blame her under the circumstances, but if she'd co-operate with Mrs. Ellis, I think she'd find Mrs. Ellis very broad-minded and very understanding.''

"Actually," Mason said, "my client was thinking of doing just that. She was thinking of going direct to Mrs. Ellis and having a heart-to-heart chat with her."

"I think that would be a wonderful thing," Gowrie said.

"No objections as Mrs. Ellis' attorney?"

"None whatever."

"All right," Mason said. "You go ahead and put on your talk to the women's club. I think I'll tell my client to go talk with Mrs. Ellis."

Mason hung up the phone, turned to Ellen Robb. "Look, Miss Robb," he said, "why don't you just go see Mrs. Ellis and tell her something of what you've told me? Don't talk too much about her husband as an individual, but talk about the problem of marriage in general. I take it you've given the subject quite a bit of thought."

"I have," she said. "I've given it thought during a lot of sleepless nights, and, believe me, that's when you really cover all the angles of a problem. Right now Mrs. Ellis may feel rather vindictive, but, believe me, it's a lot better to make sacrifices and save a marriage than to go rushing into something where you win a little alimony and then have years of loneliness to think things over."

"All right," Mason said, "you go see Mrs. Ellis and I'll get to work."

She seemed rather hurt at his brusque manner of dismissal. "I have money now, Mr. Mason. I want to pay you for your services."

Mason hesitated a moment.

"Fifty dollars," Della Street said.

Ellen Robb opened her purse, took out two twenties and a ten.

"Right this way," Della Street said. "If you'll step out to *my* office I'll give you a receipt."

"I take it you can spare that money," Mason said. "You made some sort of a settlement?"

"I received a present, Mr. Mason. It wasn't a settlement. It was for the purpose of paying my expenses in the matter and—"

"Did you sign anything?" Mason asked.

She shook her head. "George said my word is good enough for him."

Mason nodded.

"Right this way," Della Street interposed. "I'll get your receipt."

When Della had returned to the office, Mason picked up the file of urgent correspondence. "Don't you think fifty dollars was a little steep?" he asked.

"It should have been two hundred and fifty," Della Street said. "Do you realize you made a trip out of the office, killed half a day, and then she had the temerity to come back and see you? You mark my words, Chief, that girl is one who could become a pest. She's got her eye on you."

"On me?" Mason asked.

"On *you*! You don't react the way she's accustomed to having men react. You noticed the way she bent over when she leaned over to put her hands on the arm of your chair?"

"I noticed," Mason admitted.

"You were supposed to," Della Street said. "That's why she did it. I'll tell you something else. She's a pretty good shorthand stenographer. While you were talking with Gowrie over the telephone, she was taking notes."

"What!" Mason exclaimed incredulously.

"That's right."

"You're sure it was shorthand?" Mason asked.

"It was shorthand," Della Street said. "I couldn't see the point of her pencil but I could see the way her shoulder moved, and I would say she was a very clever shorthand stenographer, and she was taking down your entire conversation with Gowrie."

"Well, isn't *that* interesting," Mason said, his eyes narrowing. "And do you suppose that Mr. Gowrie called quite by accident, that the fact he made his call while Ellen Robb was in the office was pure coincidence?"

"Not pure coincidence," Della Street said flatly.

Chapter 5

Perry Mason latchkeyed the door of his private office to find Paul Drake, head of the Drake Detective Agency, visiting with Della Street over a cup of coffee from the office percolator.

"Hi, Perry," Drake said. "Della was telling me about your Rowena case."

"Quite a case," Mason said.

"Well, I'll be on my way and let you get to work. I just dropped in to make a report on that Finsley case. I gave it to Della. There's nothing you need to take any action on at the moment."

"Don't run away, Paul," Mason said. "We haven't had a visit for quite a while. I don't have anything pressing this morning."

"On the contrary," Della Street said firmly. "This is the morning you *are* going to dictate replies to the letters in that file of urgent mail. On your way, Paul."

"I've been ordered out," Paul Drake said, grinning.

He started for the door, paused midway and said to Perry Mason, "You're all cleaned up with that bunch down in Rowena?"

"Uh-huh."

"It's rather a mess down there," Drake said. "The joints actually control the town. It's a prosperous little community as far as outside money pouring in is concerned, but this fellow Anclitas you tangled with is quite a guy."

"How come?"

"I don't know too much about him," Drake said, "except that he's supposed to be bad medicine. He fights dirty. He

44

has the city attorney and the chief of police in his pocket. I don't know whether you remember reading about it, but about a year ago there was a case in the papers.''

"Involving him?''

"That's right. He filed charges against a girl who had been working there, claimed that she had been stealing money from the cash register and that she had stolen a gun. They found the gun in her possession, and she claimed the whole thing was a frame-up. There was an investigation. I guess the kid had been smoking marijuana. Quite a lot of those people connected with music go for that type of junk. The police found some marijuana in her apartment along with this stolen gun. Then George's friend, the chief of police down there, took the girl's fingerprints and from them dug up an FBI record which showed a prior conviction for marijuana.''

"What happened?'' Mason asked, interested.

"I think the girl went up, as I remember it, but she was making some wild accusations, claiming that George and his partner had framed her. Just keep an eye on those boys, Perry, and remember they've got the town all sewed up. If you have any trouble with George Anclitas, don't leave your car parked in front of a fireplug in Rowena or you'll be in jail for six months. And if they can get you where there are no witnesses, they'll charge you with resisting an officer and show bruises on *your* face to prove the charge.''

"A nice cozy little setup,'' Mason said.

"It is for a fact,'' Drake told him. "Well, I'll be on my way, Perry. I'm keeping on the job on that Finsley case. I expect to hear something definite by tomorrow. You get back to your dictation.''

"Thank you, Paul,'' Della Street said sweetly.

"I like to make him work,'' Drake said and left the office.

Perry Mason sighed, said, "One cup of coffee and one cigarette, Della.''

"All right,'' she said, "only answer those two top letters while you're sipping the coffee and smoking the cigarette.''

"Slave driver!" he charged.

Della Street adjusted her shorthand notebook on her knee. "I'm the slave," she said. "What do you want to tell that fellow?"

Della Street's phone rang while she was in the midst of taking Mason's dictation on the letter.

Della said, "Hello," listened, then cupped her hand over the mouthpiece and said to Perry Mason, "Your girl friend."

Mason raised his eyebrows.

"Ellen Robb," Della Street said.

"All right," Mason said, "we've wasted enough time with her, Della. She can't keep dropping in on us this way without an appointment. Tell Gertie to explain to her I'm busy, that I see clients only by appointment and . . . well, you'd better go out and tell her yourself. I don't want to be too obvious with the brush-off. I'm afraid this is getting to be one of those things."

"*I'll* send her on her way," Della Street said.

She pushed back her chair, walked quickly out of the office, and Mason, waiting to resume his dictation, studied the letter to which he had been replying. After some thirty seconds he began to frown impatiently. He put the letter down, took a cigarette from the silver case on the office desk and was just lighting it when Della Street returned to the office.

"Perhaps I've been uncharitable," she said.

"What is it?" Mason said.

"This time," Della Street said, "she has a story and a black eye."

"How come the black eye?"

"George."

Mason's face darkened. "I'm afraid," he said, "George needs something in the way of a lesson."

"I thought you might feel that way."

"How's she dressed?" Mason asked.

"Same outfit she had on yesterday," Della Street said, "and she'll probably lean over and put her hands on the arm of your chair. But . . . well, Chief, you have to feel sorry for

46

her. She's been batted around, and, after all, that figure of hers is her showcase. And someone has planted a gun in her baggage.''

''A gun?'' Mason asked.

Della Street nodded.

''So,'' Mason said, smiling, ''I take it you didn't send her on her way.''

Della Street shook her head. ''I told her that I thought perhaps you'd be able to see her, that you were very busy this morning and that you usually only saw people by appointment but that you *might* be able to see her. She's quite upset.''

''Let's take a look,'' Mason said. ''Bring her in. This gun business—I don't understand that. Tell her to come in. But I warn you, Della, I'm going to put her through a wringer this time.''

''The poor kid is pretty much upset,'' Della said.

''You've changed your tune quite rapidly,'' Mason observed.

''I have,'' she admitted. ''If there's anything that riles me it's the idea of these big burly men who demonstrate their manhood by hitting a good-looking girl in the eye. I hope you take this man George and put him through the hoops. After all, Miss Robb didn't sign anything, and there really wasn't any settlement within the legal meaning of the term. I think sticking George for about five thousand dollars would teach him a mighty good lesson.''

''Let's get her in,'' Mason said. ''I'm interested in the gun.''

Della Street returned to the outer office and ushered Ellen Robb into Mason's presence.

Ellen Robb tried a lopsided grin. ''Isn't it a beaut?'' she said, fingering her swollen eye.

''All right,'' Mason said, ''let's cut out the window dressing and get down to brass tacks. What happened?''

''I don't know. George was in a terrible mood last night. Every time I said anything he'd snap me up, and finally I couldn't take it any more and I told him I didn't have to. Then he really gave me a bawling out.''

"What sort of a bawling out?" Mason asked.

"I think a lawyer would refer to it as loud, vulgar and obscene language.''

"And then what?"

"Then he said something I just wouldn't take, and I slapped his face and . . . well, I have a shiner to show for it.''

"No one interfered with your packing up?"

"No one interfered with my packing up. I got out and took a taxi to another motel. This morning when I was going through my things, I looked in my bag and . . . well, there was a gun in it.''

"What sort of a gun?"

Ellen Robb opened her purse. "This," she said. "And I'm quite certain it's one of the guns he keeps there for protection. He has three or four of them by the various cash registers. This looks exactly like one of those guns. So, what do I do?"

Mason took the gun, motioned to Della Street to take her notebook. "A .38-caliber Smith & Wesson revolver with the number stamped in the metal, C 48809," he dictated.

He pushed the catch which released the cylinder, swung out the cylinder, said, "One empty cartridge case in the cylinder.''

Mason put the gun down on his desk, then after a few seconds picked it up and dropped it in his right coat pocket.

"Let's assume someone put this revolver in your bag," Mason said. "When was it done—before your altercation with George Anclitas or afterwards?"

"Before. The minute he hit me I went right to my locker and started getting my things out, then I went to my room in the motel and packed my bag.''

"Could he have gone to your room while you were getting your personal things out of your locker?"

"I suppose he could have, but somehow I don't think he

did. I don't know. I have an idea . . . it's hard to tell, Mr. Mason, but I have a definite feeling that George had decided he was going to pick a fight with me over something and get rid of me. I think the whole thing had been carefully planned and was all cut and dried.''

"Did you go and see Mrs. Ellis?''

"I tried to, but I never got to see her.''

"What do you mean, you tried?''

"They have a yacht. I rang up the house and tried to talk with her. I found she and her husband were going on a cruise and she was supposed to be aboard the yacht, getting it ready for the cruise. I went down to the yacht, but she wasn't on board.''

"Did you go out to the yacht?''''

"Yes. I got a skiff, rowed out and went around the yacht calling her name. Then I went aboard. There wasn't anyone there. I thought it over and felt that since they were going cruising together they had probably patched things up and it would be best for me to say nothing.''

"This was before your altercation with George?''

"Oh, yes, quite a bit before. The fight didn't start until nearly eleven o'clock, but I felt he was just looking for an excuse to pop me one from the minute I started to work.''

"What time did you go on duty?''

"Eight o'clock.''

Mason said, "Look here, Miss Robb, you have had stenographic training, haven't you?''

She seemed surprised. "Yes. How did you know?''

"You were taking down my conversation yesterday when I was talking on the phone.''

She flushed, seemed embarrassed, then said, "Well, yes. I—You were talking about me and . . . well, you were talking with Mrs. Ellis' lawyer, and I just wanted notes on what you said.''

Mason said, "You told me that you'd been married?''

She nodded.

"Want to talk about it?'' Mason asked.

49

"No."

"And you've been around?"

"I've been around. I'm twenty-four years old and thought I was smart. I won a beauty contest. I thought I was going to be a Hollywood actress. I had a darned good husband and I guess I just took him too much for granted. When he started getting restless and playing around, I played the jealous wife to perfection. I nagged him and made his home life a hell. I drove him right into her arms. I told you that before."

"And then?" Mason asked.

"Then," she said, "I just didn't seem to care. I went out and tried to get away from everything and everybody I knew. I found that *good* stenographic jobs were rather difficult to get. I got a job as hat-check girl in The Green Swan. We only got to keep a very small percentage of our tips there, and George had his eye on me. He found out I liked to sing and he offered me a good job with a salary and a chance to keep all my tips—Look, Mr. Mason, your time is valuable. If I tried to tell you about all of my career, you'd have to charge me more than I could afford to pay."

"Have you ever had any trouble with the law?"

"Never."

Mason turned to Della Street, said, "If you'll excuse us, Miss Robb, I have to make a rather confidential phone call at this time." Mason walked around his desk, opened the door to the law library and nodded to Della Street.

She joined him and Mason pulled the door shut.

"Well?" Della asked.

"I don't like it," Mason said. "I have a feeling that I've been suckered into a trap."

"By Ellen Robb?" she asked.

"By George Anclitas," Mason said, "and I don't like it."

"What do you think happened?"

"George resented me when I first appeared on the scene Monday morning. He realized, however, that I had him in a position where he was hooked, and struggling or resentment

50

wouldn't do him any good, so he capitalized on my weakness."

"Your weakness?" Della Street asked.

"Exactly," Mason said. "I should have been a hardboiled lawyer. I should have made a settlement on behalf of my client, charged her thirty-three and a third per cent of it and had proper releases signed. In place of that, I left it to her to make her own terms with George so she wouldn't have to pay me any fee, and I walked out.

"That's where George saw a heaven-sent opportunity. He started playing up to Miss Robb. He ate a little crow and told her he was sorry. He got her to stay on. All the time he was planning to jockey her into a position where she'd be in trouble, and if I tried to help her I'd be in trouble."

"The gun?" she asked.

"I think in due time he's going to charge her with stealing the gun. He may even plant some dope in her baggage."

"When do you think George will spring this trap of his?" Della asked.

"When I have filed an action on behalf of Ellen Robb."

"You intend to do that?"

"Sure I intend to do that. I have to, to protect her interests and to save my own face. The point is, Della, that I started something that is destined to raise the devil with the gambling interests. They aren't going to like that. They're going to try to smear me in some way, and Ellen Robb is their point of contact.

"You can see from the way she tells her story that they laid plans very carefully and then George punched her in the eye."

"She slapped his face," Della pointed out.

"He egged her on," Mason said.

The lawyer was thoughtful for a few minutes, then he said, "Della, we've got quite a collection of guns in the safe, guns that have been surrendered by clients from time to time. Do you suppose we have a Smith & Wesson in there—one of the police models with a two-and-a-half-inch barrel?"

"Yes, I'm certain we do."

"Get the gun and bring it in here," Mason said.

Della Street went to the safe and after some two minutes returned with the gun.

The lawyer extracted one of the cartridges, pried the bullet out, shook out the powder, put the empty cartridge shell back in the revolver and, going over to the coat closet, exploded the percussion cap with the hammer. He replaced the other cartridges, put the revolver in his left coat pocket and returned to the office.

"I'm sorry we had to keep you waiting, Miss Robb," he said.

"It's all right."

"Is Ellen Robb your true name or a professional name?"

"Let's put it this way, Mr. Mason, Ellen Robb is as near my real name as you or anyone else will ever know. The man I was once married to has become a big businessman now. I wouldn't drag his name into . . . into the sort of work I'm doing."

"Where were you intending to go?" Mason asked, absently lighting a cigarette.

"I want to take a bus to Arizona. I have an offer of a job at Phoenix. A girl that I know has the photographic concession in a night club, and there's an opening for a girl to sell cigars, cigarettes and double as a hat-check girl. But what do I do about the gun?"

Mason reached in his left pocket, took out the gun he had placed there, weighed it in his hand as though debating what was to be done with the weapon. "I don't like to have you turn it in to the police," he said. "It seems to me that . . . well, I don't know . . . after all, we don't want to borrow trouble."

The lawyer pushed the gun toward her and said, "Perhaps you'd better keep it, Ellen. Remember that you showed it to us and told us about it."

"Shall I keep it in my purse?"

"Heavens no. You don't have a permit," Mason said. "Put it back in your bag where you found it."

"And what shall I do with it?"

"Keep it for evidence," Mason told her. "You have no idea how it got in your bag?"

"No idea whatever."

"Well, you've done everything you can. I'm going to file suit against Anclitas. Where are you staying?"

"Unit 19, the Surf and Sea Motel at Costa Mesa."

"Go back to your motel. I want to know where you are at all times. If you leave there, let me know."

"If you're going to file a suit, you'll want some more money," she said. "This is—"

Mason shook his head. "No more money. Not unless something else turns up. We're all fixed. Save your money until I ask for it.

"Go back to the motel and wait. By the way, what about Helman Ellis? Was he there when you and George were having this altercation?"

"No."

"You said you had heard he and his wife were going on a cruise. Do you know if they actually went?"

"I don't know. Helly was in The Big Barn last night before the altercation with George. He said his wife had marooned him aboard the yacht. They'd had a fight."

"Keep in touch with me," Mason said. "I want to know right where I can reach you."

She impulsively gave him her hand. "Thank you, Mr. Mason," she said. "I'll never forget this."

"I probably won't myself," Mason said.

Della Street ushered her to the door, shook hands with her, returned to the office.

"Did you switch guns?" she asked.

"I switched guns," Mason said.

"And she has no idea?"

"I hope not," Mason said. "I hope I wasn't crude—Just

53

where did that gun I gave her come from, Della? What about it?''

"According to our records," Della Street said, "that gun is a .38 Smith & Wesson Special with the number 133347. You may remember that when George Spencer Ranger came to us and wanted you to represent him, you asked him if he carried a gun. He said he always carried one, that he didn't have a permit because he didn't need one, that he'd been appointed a deputy sheriff in Arizona. You told him that he'd better leave the gun with us. This is the gun that he gave us.''

"All right," Mason said. "Give this other gun to Paul Drake. Tell him to first trace the registration, then take it to Maurice Halstead, the ballistics expert who does his work. Tell Halstead to fire some test bullets through it and save the bullets. Then bring the gun back here. You can lock it in the safe.

"Then, when George Anclitas swears to a complaint charging Ellen Robb with stealing one of his guns, gets a search warrant and finds a gun in her baggage, he'll naturally assume his little scheme is working perfectly.''

"Then you'll jerk the rug out from under him?" Della asked.

"Then I'll jerk the rug."

"But what about this gun that was planted in Ellen Robb's baggage?''

Mason grinned. "If Paul Drake's investigation shows that it's George Anclitas' gun, it will be right back in George Anclitas' place of business and no one can ever prove it had been missing.''

"Is that legal?''

Mason said, "I know of no law which keeps one from returning lost property to the owner.''

Chapter 6

When Della Street had returned from Paul Drake's office, after leaving the gun with him, Mason said, "Let's get Gowrie on the phone, Della. I want to see how *he's* feeling this morning."

Della Street put through the call, nodded to Perry Mason.

Mason picked up the telephone, said, "Hello, Gowrie. Perry Mason speaking."

"Oh, yes, Mr. Mason. How are you today?"

"Pretty good. My secretary and I want to sit in on your talk to the women's club at Rowena, Gowrie. We may have some trouble getting in, but if you would invite us as your guests we probably wouldn't have any trouble."

Gowrie hesitated a moment.

"You there?" Mason asked.

"I'm here," Gowrie said. "I was just trying to marshal my thoughts."

"What about your thoughts?" Mason said. "Why do they need marshaling?"

"I am not going to make the talk at Rowena."

"You're not?"

"No."

"Why not?"

"Well, for one thing, Mrs. Ellis hasn't completed the arrangements that she had agreed on."

"What do you mean?"

"I was to receive a fee from the women's club for the talk, and there was to be a retainer in connection with her case."

"She hasn't paid anything?"

"Not a cent. And I can't reach her. I can't find her. Apparently she went yachting. Under the circumstances, I rang up the president of the Rowena Women's Club and told her that the talk would have to be postponed.''

''Like that, eh?'' Mason asked.

''Like that,'' Gowrie said. ''You know how it is yourself, Counselor. A lawyer can't go around giving his services away.''

''All right,'' Mason said. ''Let me know when you hear from Mrs. Ellis, will you?''

Mason hung up the phone. ''Did you listen in on that, Della?''

She nodded.

''Well,'' Mason said, ''I guess there's nothing much to be done at the present time.''

''Except that mail file,'' she said. ''We still haven't got at those important letters.''

Mason sighed, picked up the mail file and spent the rest of the day in dictation.

In the late afternoon Paul Drake's code knock sounded on the door.

Della Street got up to let him in.

Paul Drake stretched himself out on the big overstuffed chair in the lawyer's office and said, ''What the hell have you been doing, Perry, juggling guns again?''

''Why the again?'' Mason asked.

Drake said, ''I don't know, but any time you get in a case and a gun figures in it, you certainly seem to play three-card monte with the prosecution and the police.''

''Anything wrong with that?'' Mason asked.

''Not if you get away with it,'' Drake said.

''And what brings up all those remarks?'' Mason asked.

''That gun you wanted me to trace—a .38 Smith & Wesson number C 48809.''

''What about it?''

''It's one of four guns that were purchased, all on the same date, by W. W. Marcus, full name Wilton Winslow Marcus. He's supposed to be some sort of a silent partner of George

Anclitas in a restaurant deal in Rowena. The restaurant is mostly a front for gambling.''

"Permit?" Mason asked.

"Apparently no permit. They own the chief of police at Rowena. He appointed them some sort of special officers. Apparently both Anclitas and Marcus are specials. That gives them an opportunity to carry firearms without any written permit other than their authorization as special officers."

"And this gun is one of the four that were purchased?"

Drake nodded.

"All right. What else?" Mason asked.

"I had a ballistics expert fire test bullets from it and then replace the cartridges that were in the gun just as they were when you handed them to me."

"And the test bullets have all been marked for identification?"

Drake nodded.

"Okay," Mason said. "Where's the gun?"

Drake took the gun from his pocket and handed it to Mason. "You be careful you don't get into trouble with that," Drake said.

"What sort of trouble, Paul?"

"Darned if I know, but . . . you evidently have the idea the gun has been used in committing some sort of a crime."

"What gives you *that* idea?"

"Otherwise, why would you want test bullets fired from it?"

"Perhaps," Mason said, "I merely wanted to date the gun."

"What do you mean by that, Perry?"

Mason opened the drawer of his desk, took out a piece of steel that was bent at the end into a small, sharp point, said, "This is a tool for etching steel, Paul."

Mason inserted the tool in the barrel of the gun, drew it along the length of the barrel, then inserted it once more and again drew the tool along the length of the gun barrel.

"What's the idea?" Drake asked.

Mason said, "If we fire a bullet through that gun now, there will be striations that are in addition to and different from those of the test bullets that have previously been fired through it. Is that right?"

"If you want to be sure, better make a couple of more marks," Drake said.

Mason repeated the process of scratching the barrel. "How's that?"

"That should do it very nicely," Drake said.

Mason opened the drawer of his desk and dropped the gun down in the drawer.

Drake regarded him thoughtfully. "You know, there's a law about tampering with evidence."

"Evidence of what?" Mason asked.

"I don't know," Drake said.

Mason grinned. "We're not supposed to be clairvoyant, Paul. If you adopt that attitude, you could never change anything in connection with any object. You couldn't even tear up a piece of paper and throw it away. You couldn't wash a dirty dish. You'd be altering or destroying evidence. Any object doesn't become evidence until you know or have reason to believe that it has become identified with a crime in some manner."

"And you have no reason to believe that this gun is connected with a crime?"

"Very definitely not," Mason said. "I am simply protecting a client."

"And that will protect the client?" Drake asked.

"It may help," Mason said. "I'm sitting in a game where I don't know what cards have been played and moreover I don't know what are trumps. But we've been dealt a hand. It may not be a very good hand. It probably was dealt to us from a cold deck with the idea that it was the lowest hand in the deck. I've got to play that hand so it becomes a winning hand."

"Without knowing trumps and without knowing what cards have already been played?"

"That's right."

"That's a job you can have," Drake said. "I'm glad I'm not a lawyer. Anything else before I go home, Perry?"

"Not right now."

Drake got to his feet, moved lazily toward the door, paused at the entrance door to look back at Mason. "This deal in Rowena could be bad business," he said. "There's a lot of money involved."

"That's right," Mason said.

Drake hesitated a moment longer, then shrugged his shoulders, opened the door and walked out.

Della Street looked at Mason and raised her eyebrows in silent inquiry.

"Now then," Mason said, "we know this gun is the property of George Anclitas. I want to get it back to his place of business. We have to—"

The lawyer was interrupted by the ringing of the telephone.

"That's Gertie," Mason said. "See what it is, Della."

Della Street picked up the telephone, said, "Yes, Gertie," then said, "Just a minute." She looked at Mason. "Mr. Helman Ellis is in the outer office and says it is very important that he get in touch with you at the earliest possible moment. He realizes it's after office hours but he wants to know if you can see him immediately."

Mason hesitated a moment, appraising the situation, then said, "I'll see him immediately, Della. Go out and bring him in."

Della Street said, "I'll be right out, Gertie," and hung up the phone.

"Go through the usual routine," Mason instructed her. "Get his name, address, telephone number where he can be reached, and then bring him in."

Della nodded, then walked out through the doorway to the reception room.

A few minutes later she returned and said, "Mr. Mason, Mr. Ellis."

Mason got up to shake hands.

Ellis was a tall individual in his late twenties. He had high cheekbones, a somewhat Slavic cast of features, a long, thin mouth, steady blue eyes. He was big-boned and wrapped powerful fingers around Mason's hand as the two men shook hands.

"Sit down," Mason said. "Is there anything I can do for you?"

"I don't know," Ellis said. "It depends on how you're tied up."

"I am representing Ellen Robb."

"That's why I'm here," Ellis said.

"What is your trouble?"

"My wife."

"I don't take divorce cases," Mason said. "I try to specialize pretty much in trial work. A good deal of my practice is criminal cases. Domestic relations, contracts and all that just don't appeal to me."

"My wife," Ellis said simply, "is going to kill your client."

Mason raised his eyebrows.

"There is no real cause for jealousy," Ellis said, "but my wife has in my opinion become temporarily insane."

Mason said, "Let's get certain facts straight. You have been playing a lot of poker at The Big Barn and you've lost rather heavily?"

"That's right."

"Your wife didn't take kindly to the idea?"

"Wives don't take kindly to the idea of husbands sitting in poker games and losing money."

"And Ellen Robb was rather conspicuous around The Big Barn?"

"They made her conspicuous," Ellis said.

"And you became interested in her?"

Ellis took a deep breath and said, "Mr. Mason, I love her."

"And yet you say your wife has no reason to be jealous?"

"I'll put it this way, Mr. Mason. I hadn't—I have been keeping it to myself."

"You mean you think you've been keeping it to yourself," Mason said.

"What do you mean by that?"

"A wife can smell a situation of that sort a mile away," Mason said. "If you're in love with Ellen Robb, you can rest assured that your wife knew there was something more to your excursions to The Big Barn than a desire to sit in a poker game."

"She doesn't know how I really feel," Ellis said, "because it was only recently I faced the situation myself and realized I had fallen in love."

"She knew it before you did," Mason said, "otherwise, why should she have become so jealous?"

"She's always been jealous. She's jealous of any woman that I look at twice."

"Have you looked at many women twice?"

"Not much more than that."

"All right. Tell me what happened."

"Well, I knew that Nadine, my wife, was building up to terrific emotional tension. I'd lost some money playing poker but I could afford to lose money playing poker. Then she made a scene. You know all about that—that was one thing I couldn't afford, to be branded as a welsher.

"Mr. Mason, if Nadine had filed suit against George Anclitas on account of money that I lost playing poker, I would be branded from coast to coast as a piker, a welsher."

"Suppose the game was crooked?"

"That, of course, is different. If anyone could *prove* the game was crooked, the situation would be different."

"All right. What happened?" Mason asked. "Let's get down to brass tacks."

"I learned that my wife had made a scene down at The Big Barn. I learned that you had given her some legal authorities which would enable her to try to recover the money I had lost. I learned that she had gone to an attorney and retained him to file suit. So I told Nadine that we simply had to talk things out. We decided to go on a cruise on my yacht. We would be uninterrupted that way. We could sail out beyond the harbor and try to get the whole thing settled. We'd done that once or twice before during periods of crisis in our married life, and things had worked out all right."

"How long have you been married?" Mason asked.

"Seven years."

"All right, go on. What happened?"

"We left the house," Ellis said, "to go to the yacht. We told the neighbors that we would probably be out all night or perhaps two nights. We planned to sleep on the yacht. We planned to have dinner on the yacht. We stopped to buy some provisions.

"It seems that almost immediately after we left the house, Ellen showed up. She wanted to talk to my wife. The neighbor told her we were down on the yacht so Ellen went down there, rented a skiff and rowed out to where the yacht was moored. She rowed all around it and called out several times. Then she tied up the skiff and went aboard. When she didn't find anyone there, she took the skiff and rowed back to the place where she had rented the skiff.

"Now, that was the last straw that touched everything off. While Ellen was on the yacht, she apparently had dropped a handkerchief that had her name embroidered in the corner. We got aboard the yacht and went down to the cabin and . . . well, my wife found Ellen's handkerchief.

"That really started things going. My wife was frantic. She wouldn't listen to anything I had to say.

"Of course, at the time I had no way of knowing how Ellen's handkerchief got aboard the yacht. I thought somebody had planted it. I tried to tell my wife that it was simply a scheme by which someone was trying to discredit me, and perhaps it was something the gamblers had done to get her mind off the idea of recovering some of the money I had lost gambling."

"What happened?"

"Nadine was crazy. Mr. Mason, she just went temporarily insane. She took the gun—"

"What gun?" Mason asked.

"A revolver that we keep aboard the yacht for protection when we're at sea or when we're sleeping aboard the yacht while its moored in the harbor."

"You don't carry a gun?"

"No. We kept a gun there on the yacht. That was the only place I thought we might ever need one. I understand that sometimes there have been holdups on some of the yachts that were moored in the harbor—vicious young thugs who get aboard a yacht and commit all sorts of atrocities—tie up the men, submit the women to indignities, take money and all of that."

"What sort of a gun?" Mason asked.

"A revolver."

"Do you know the make?"

"Smith & Wesson."

"Where did you get it?"

"It was a present."

"Who gave it to you?"

"George."

"George Anclitas?"

"Yes."

"Do you know the number that was on the gun?"

"Heavens no!"

"How did George happen to give you the gun?"

"Well, George and I have been rather friendly over a period of several weeks. I like to play cards and . . . well, we played with varying results. Sometimes I'd win, sometimes George would win, and we became friendly. I happened to see this gun when George and his partner were discussing firearms. They had made some sort of a bet about it. George explained that he kept several guns around the place so that in case of a holdup there would be more than one person who could get his hands on a gun. I told him I was thinking of getting a gun for the yacht because I'd read about a situation where a group of three thugs had boarded a yacht and tied the owner up and . . . well, he pressed the gun on me, told me to take it.''

"Where is that gun now?''

"I told you. Nadine has it.''

"All right, she took the gun,'' Mason said. "What happened after she took the gun?''

"She told me that if I wanted to have a rendezvous aboard the yacht with my paramour, she wasn't going to stand for it. She told me that she was going to invoke the unwritten law and kill Ellen. It was a terrible scene. I have never seen her like that before. She was utterly insane.''

"What did she do?''

"Got in the skiff and rowed away and left me marooned on the yacht.''

"Didn't you object to that?''

"Of course I objected to it. If I could have got close enough, Mr. Mason, I'd have knocked her down and taken the gun away, but she was too smart for that. She made me keep my distance and she kept me covered. I believe she would have killed me. In fact, the idea in her mind at that time was to kill me aboard the yacht, then kill Ellen and then kill herself.''

"But why leave you marooned aboard the yacht?''

"She was afraid I would try to warn Ellen.''

"Go on,'' Mason said. "What happened?''

"That's about all I know. She rowed away in the skiff. I was marooned aboard the yacht until nearly nine-thirty. Then I was able to attract the attention of a party of yachtsmen and got taken ashore.''

"Couldn't you have started the engine on the yacht and gone into the pier?''

"No chance,'' Ellis said. "She took the keys to the starting switch with her. I had had a burglarproof lock put on there so that when the keys are out it's impossible to start the motor. I suppose an electrician could have short-circuited the wires back of the locking mechanism but I didn't know how to do it and I'm not too certain it could have been done. I had the sort of lock installed that would keep people from stealing the yacht and taking it for a joy ride.

"It's not a particularly large yacht, Mr. Mason; only forty-two feet, but it's very expensive and perfectly appointed. I have spent a lot of money trying to make it very comfortable."

"All right," Mason said, "you got ashore about nine-thirty. Then what?"

"So then I tried to find my wife and I couldn't find her. I went to talk with Ellen but I didn't want to alarm her. I just told her to be careful, that my wife was on the warpath. So then I went out looking for Nadine."

"Then this morning my wife showed up very briefly at the house. She made further threats. She said Ellen Robb had been meeting me secretly aboard the yacht, that she was going to prove that fact by having fingerprint experts develop her latent fingerprints.

"She also said she felt Ellen was waiting for me on the yacht right then and that if she was, she was going to kill her."

"What did you do then?"

"Nothing. Ellen had never met me aboard the yacht. I knew Nadine was barking up the wrong tree, so I let her go . . . But I want you to know that my wife is in a murderous rage so that you can take steps to protect Ellen."

"Did you know that Ellen Robb and George Anclitas had had an altercation?"

"What about the altercation?"

"He fired her, and gave her a black eye to boot," Mason said.

"What!" Ellis exclaimed, half rising from the chair.

"Gave her a black eye," Mason said.

Ellis said, "I'll kill him for that. That . . . that boorish, arrogant, crooked . . ."

Ellis quit talking, compressed his lips in a thin, straight line.

Mason said, "On behalf of Miss Robb I'm filing suit against George Anclitas and several John Does, who I think are partners in the business, for six thousand dollars exemplary damages and fifteen hundred dollars actual damages for pain and suffering."

Ellis said, "Mr. Mason, I am beginning to be satisfied that game was crooked. I think that . . . I think that Ellen could tell you something about that. I want to get even with George Anclitas. If he struck Ellen, I'm going to give him the beating of his life. I'll—"

"And how will that look when your wife files suit for divorce and names Ellen Robb as correspondent?" Mason asked.

Ellis' face showed dismay.

"There are some things you have to take into consideration," Mason said dryly.

"Look," Ellis said, "I'll do anything I can in this matter, Mason. I'll—I'd like to pay your fees for prosecuting that case against George."

"And how would *that* look in the divorce action?" Mason asked.

Ellis hesitated, then said, "All right. I have lost around ten thousand dollars there in The Big Barn. I'm now satisfied the game was crooked. If you want to act as my attorney to recover that money, I'll pay you fifty per cent of the recovery and give you all the expense money you need to prosecute. You can hire detectives or do anything else you need to do."

"I may be disqualified on that action," Mason said. "I already advised your wife—gratuitously, of course—that she could probably recover the community funds that had been lost gambling, regardless of whether the game was straight or crooked."

"Mr. Mason, don't you understand what that would do to my reputation? I'd be the laughingstock of—"

"I don't think so," Mason interrupted. "I think if a few women would take action of this sort, it would give the big

66

gamblers something to think about, particularly the ones where the games are crooked.''

"On the contrary," Ellis said with some feeling. "It would have exactly the opposite effect, Mr. Mason. The ones who were running square games couldn't afford to stay in business. If they were faced with the prospect of having to give up their winnings when some woman filed suit claiming it was community property that the husband had lost, the ones who were running a straight game would find that the percentage was too much against them and they'd go out of business. On the other hand, the crooked gamblers would stay in business. Or I'll put it this way. The gamblers who stayed in business would be crooked.''

"You have a point there," Mason said. "I don't know, of course, what's going to happen when the doctrine laid down in this decision is tested in the Supreme Court of this state or the Supreme Court of the United States. This, however, is at present a new angle on the law of community property. It's an interesting legal development, and I'm going to watch and see what happens.''

"Well, I'll say one thing," Ellis said. "You certainly threw a monkey wrench into the City of Rowena. George would do almost anything to keep that information from being made public. I guess you know that my wife intended to have a meeting and retained an attorney by the name of Gowrie to address the meeting, and George promptly bought him off.''

Mason raised his eyebrows. "Bought him off?''

"Sure he did. Oh, nothing crude. He didn't go to Gowrie and offer him money not to appear at the meeting, but Gowrie now has some new clients who brought him some rather important business and I think conveyed the idea to him that they would be very unhappy if he addressed a meeting of the Women's Club of Rowena on the subject of gambling.''

"He told me," Mason said, "that he couldn't get hold of your wife.''

"Sure, he was trying to reach her but he was trying to reach her to tell her that he'd have to postpone the meeting and that he didn't think he'd be available. I think he also was going to tell her that after thinking the matter over and looking up the law on the subject, he had decided that the point probably wasn't well taken.''

"How do you know all this?"

"He talked with me on the telephone. He was feeling his way," Ellis said.

"All right," Mason told him. "I'll think over the information you've given me. If you get in touch with your wife, let me know at once."

"Tell me, Mason, is Ellen in a safe place? That's what I want to know. Can you guarantee protection?"

"I can't guarantee protection to anyone," Mason said.

"How about the police?"

"They can't either," Mason said. "If the police tried to put guards around every woman who is threatened with death at the hands of a jealous spouse, they wouldn't have enough officers left to direct traffic."

"But she's in actual danger."

"That may be," Mason said. "She is, however, fairly well concealed. I'm going to keep her under cover for the time being and I appreciate the information you've given me."

"However, these things happen. You pick up the paper almost any day and you'll find where some jealous ex-husband went to the apartment of his divorced wife, made a scene, killed her and killed himself. Or where a woman threatened to leave her husband, and he told her that if he couldn't have her, no one else was going to and pulled out a gun and killed her, then gave himself up to the authorities. These crimes of emotion account for the majority of our murders, but for every person who is actually killed under circumstances of that sort, there are a thousand who are threatened. The police simply can't cope with any situation of that sort."

"You sound cold-blooded about it," Ellis said heatedly. "Ellen Robb is a beautiful woman, a sweet, good, young woman. Oh, I know she's been around, but essentially she's a mighty fine, sweet young woman and . . . well, you simply can't sit back and let my wife go all out on the warpath this way.''

''Where do you think your wife is now?''

''I think she's in Arizona. The story was that Ellen was to get a job at one of the night clubs in Phoenix. She had some connections there, and I suppose that's where Nadine went. If Ellen is here, I certainly hope Nadine is in Arizona—I'm hoping she'll cool down by the time she gets back.''

''Well, we'll see what we can do,'' Mason said. ''I'll try and protect my client to the best of my ability, but you understand we can't furnish absolute protection in a situation of that sort; even the police can't.''

Ellis said, ''Look here, Mr. Mason, if the police can't protect her, we can hire a private bodyguard for her. I want to pay for it, no matter what it costs. Armed guards who can watch her day and night.''

''And how will *that* look in the divorce suit?'' Mason asked.

Ellis thought over the lawyer's remark. ''I guess I'm licked,'' he said, getting to his feet. ''However, Mr. Mason, I'm telling you there's a real danger to your client and to me.''

Mason merely nodded.

Ellis seemed reluctant to leave the office, but Mason arose, signifying the interview was terminated.

As soon as Ellis left the office, Mason nodded to Della Street. ''Get Paul Drake, if he hasn't already gone home, Della. Have him come down here right away.''

Less than a minute later, Drake was in Mason's office.

Mason said, ''Ellen Robb is staying at the Surf and Sea Motel in Costa Mesa. She's registered under her real name. She may or may not be in some danger. Apparently an irate wife is on the warpath and is looking for her with a gun.''

''Bodyguard?'' Drake asked.

''Bodyguards,'' Mason said, ''the 's' sound signifies the

plural, two or more, and without her knowing anything about it. I want you to keep an eye on the place. Have men on duty down there where they can watch the door of Ellen Robb's motel apartment. If any woman asks for Ellen or if any woman shows up, have your men get on the job. If the woman is about twenty-seven, red-haired, streamlined, perhaps a little on the thinnish side, I want your man to stop her, no matter on what pretext, and if her name should be Nadine Ellis—Mrs. Helman Ellis—I want your men to take some action."

"How much action?"

"It depends on the circumstances," Mason said. "Divert her attention and . . . well, in any event, stick right with her. If this woman sees Ellen Robb, I want at least one of your men there. I want him to make certain there isn't any opportunity for Mrs. Ellis to pull a gun and go bang, bang."

"I get it," Drake said. "We do a lot of that stuff. I've got some pretty good men. However, it runs into money. How long do you want them kept on the job?"

"As long as there's any possibility of trouble," Mason said.

"How long will that be?"

"Until we locate Mrs. Ellis and find out more about the situation."

"Okay," Drake said. "Will do."

After Drake had left, Mason turned to Della Street. "Now," he said, "we have the question of the gun."

"How do you mean?"

"We start out with four guns that George Anclitas had," Mason said. "He gave one away. That leaves three. Now, one of them shows up in the personal effects of Ellen Robb. Presumably, George is going to claim that gun was stolen from him. That leaves George with two guns."

"What are you getting at?" Della Street asked.

"Simply trying to keep the guns straight," Mason said, grinning. "Usually when I get in a case the district attorney

70

accuses me of introducing additional guns and juggling them around and—"

"And that's exactly what you've done in this case," Della Street said.

"I have, for a fact. Won't it be nice when George Anclitas 'discovers' that one of his guns has been stolen and accuses Ellen Robb of having committed the theft? He'll get a search warrant for her baggage. Then the officers will discover the gun, and then George will swear to a complaint. The matter will be brought into court and when they start introducing the gun in evidence, I'll ask that the number of the gun be read into evidence. Then we'll check the records to get the numbers of George's gun and then it will turn out that the gun that was found in Ellen's baggage wasn't the gun that was 'stolen' from George Anclitas."

"And then?" Della asked, smiling.

Mason grinned gleefully. "Then," he said, "We'll have another suit for damages against George Anclitas. Perhaps after a while, Della, we'll teach him not to pick on women and black their eyes."

"But," Della Street asked, "suppose someone finds you're holding George's gun up here?"

"Why, the very idea!" Mason exclaimed. "I wouldn't *think* of holding George's gun up here. I told you we were going to return it to the owner as soon as we knew who the owner was."

"You'll just hand it to him?" she asked, her eyes twinkling.

"I said we'd *return* it," Mason answered, grinning.

"Do you have a plan?" she asked.

Mason said, "Downstairs at the soda fountain they use ice in the drinks that is round, about an inch diameter with a hole in the center and—"

"Go ahead," Della Street said, as Mason broke off and started to chuckle.

"I think," Mason said, "they make that ice around the outside of a pipe. They have some process by which they fill

71

a larger pipe with water, freeze it, then get the ice out in lengths and cut it into pieces to put in the drinks.

"Suppose you run down, Della, talk with whoever is in charge and find out if you can get a piece of ice about . . . oh, say twelve inches long."

Della Street regarded him quizzically for a moment, then smiled and said, "On my way, Counselor. I take it we're about to freeze the evidence."

"On the contrary," Mason said. "We're going to melt a hard heart. Also, Della, pick up a shoe box and fill it half full of dry ice."

Della Street nodded, left the office.

Mason was once more pacing the floor when Della Street returned with a shoe box under her arm.

"Get it?" Mason asked.

She nodded.

She reached in the shoe box which contained dry ice and pulled out a twelve-inch cylinder of ice.

"All right," Mason said. "We'll try it for strength."

The lawyer took the gun which Ellen Robb had brought with her, ran the tube of ice through the trigger guard, then moved up two chairs and suspended the revolver between the two chairs, the cylinder of ice resting on the back of each one.

"Perfect!" he said, quickly removed the tube of ice and put it back in the box containing the dry ice.

"Now what?" Della Street asked.

"Now," Mason said, "we go down to Rowena. I stop on the block back of The Big Barn, where there's an entrance to the motel. You get out, walk through the motel, around the swimming pool and into The Big Barn by the back entrance. You go to the women's powder room—"

"Carrying this shoe box?" Della Street asked.

Mason shook his head. "You'll be carrying a purse by that time. The purse will be filled with dry ice, this tube of ice and the gun. We'll also stuff the hollow of ice with dry ice. You go into the women's powder room and look for

72

a place to plant the gun, either high up by suspending the gun from two corners of a partition, or preferably, if you can find a washbowl that has open plumbing underneath it, and I think you can, you can suspend the two ends of the ice tube from the two shut-off valves which you'll find underneath; one on the hot water, one on the cold water pipes.''

"And then?'' she asked.

"Then after a period of time, depending on temperature, the ice tube melts enough so the gun drops down to the floor. The ice will melt into a pool of water, and someone will find the gun on the floor.''

"And they'll connect it with us?'' Della Street asked.

"If you do it right,'' Mason said, "and go in from the back entrance this early in the evening, no one is going to see you. I don't like to ask it of you, Della, but I am an attorney of record now with interests adverse to George Anclitas, and it's not ethical for me to talk with him except in the presence of his attorney. If I should go there, he'll want to talk with me. And I want the gun found in the women's powder room.''

"Why there?'' she asked.

"Because there's an attendant there,'' Mason said, "and because it's right near the back door which leads to the motel. You can pop in there, wait until some other woman comes in, plant the ice tube, give the attendant a quarter and leave the place. You can rejoin me in the car. We'll have stuffed the hole in this ice with dry ice, which will keep it from melting for some little time. When the gun falls to the floor, either the attendant will see it, or some woman who is in the place will see it within a few minutes after it has fallen. If we're lucky, the attendant will swear the gun couldn't possibly have been there over four or five minutes.''

"And we'll be long gone?'' Della Street asked.

"We'll be long gone,'' Mason said.

"How much of a crime am I committing?''

"I've told you," Mason said, "we're returning lost property. That's highly commendable."

"How about suppressing evidence?"

"Evidence of what?"

"Of theft."

"I didn't steal anything," Mason said.

"How about Ellen Rob?"

"She's a client."

"She's a client," Della Street said thoughtfully, "but don't go overboard on that girl. She knows which side of the bread has the butter and she doesn't intend to have anyone give her bread that isn't buttered."

Mason grinned. "Meaning, perhaps, that she might butter up people?"

"Particularly her lawyer," Della Street said. "I wish you'd play this one close to your chest, Chief."

Mason nodded. "That's why I want to get that gun back where it belongs."

"What will George Anclitas think when the gun is reported as having been found in the women's powder room?"

"That, of course, depends," Mason said, "on what he's planning to do."

"You think George Anclitas intends to file charges of theft against Ellen?"

Mason's forehead puckered into a frown. "I wish I knew the answer to that, Della," he said. "I certainly thought that was what he had in mind when he planted the gun in Ellen's suitcase, but why is he holding his fire? He's waiting for something. What is it?"

"Perhaps waiting to find out where she is," Della Street said.

"I doubt it—and there's one thing that bothers me."

"What?"

"Suppose he's playing a much deeper game than that?"

"What could it be?"

"I don't know," Mason said, "but I want to get that

gun back into his possession. I want it planted in the women's powder room. The attendant there will find it. In all probability she's frightened to death of a gun. She'll cause something of a commotion and . . . well, George will know he's got his gun back."

"Of course he'll suspect you," Mason said. "And he'll also conclude that he waited too long before lowering the boom on Ellen Robb, that she found the gun in her suitcase and managed to return it. George will naturally be furious."

"When do we go?" Della Street asked.

Mason said, "You go down to the shop that sells handbags, on the corner, and get a leather handbag in which you can stuff the dry ice, the gun and the tube of ice. Then we're on our way."

Chapter 7

Perry Mason eased the car to a stop.

"Everything okay, Della?"

Della Street put her hand on the catch of the door. "Everything okay."

"Now, look," Mason said, "there's just a chance something may go wrong at either end of the line. If anything goes wrong with you, if anybody catches you, you send for me. I'll come in and we'll face it. I'll state that you were acting under my instructions, that I was returning a gun that had been planted in my client's baggage. We'll take it from there.

"Now, get that straight, Della. I don't want you to try this on your own. If anything goes wrong, you just step back out of the picture and I step in and take the responsibility. Understand?"

She hesitated a moment, then nodded.

"Now, those are instructions," Mason said. "*Don't* try to take the responsibility if you get into a jam. Now, here's the other situation. Something may go wrong out here. Someone may spot me.

"I'm going to drive around the block, into the alley and turn my lights on. If you see my lights on, everything is clear. You come on out and get in the car. . . . You can see those lights from the end of the swimming pool there.

"If, however, anything goes wrong, I won't have my lights on. If you come to the end of the swimming pool and see that my lights are off, don't come anywhere near the car. Understand?"

"For how long?" she asked.

"Until you see the car in the alley with the lights on. Then come across and join me."

"And if it's a long time, say over half an hour?"

"Under those circumstances," Mason said, "get back the best way you can. Take a bus or hitchhike."

"Okay," she said, "I'm on my way."

She opened the car door, slid out to the sidewalk, crossed the sidewalk and walked past the entrance to the motel around back of the swimming pool.

Mason circled the block to the left, came to the alley, drove down the alley until he was in a position where he could see the end of the swimming pool, then shut off his motor and waited, with his lights on.

So intent was the lawyer on watching the swimming pool that he failed to keep an eye on the rearview mirror and did not see the car which pulled up behind him.

Two men got out and walked up to where Mason was sitting.

Miles Overton, the chief of police, said, "This is the lawyer I was telling you about."

Mason snapped to quick attention, turned and said casually, "Hello, Chief."

"Want you to meet a friend of mine," the chief said. "This is Ralston Fenwick, Mr. Mason."

A heavy-set, bullnecked individual with smiling lips and cold green eyes extended a pudgy hand on which a scintillating diamond made sparks of fire. "How are you, Mr. Mason? Mighty glad to know you."

"What are you doing here?" the chief asked.

"Parking," Mason said wearily, switching off the lights on his car. "Looking over the lay of the land. I want to make a diagram of the premises."

"How come?" the chief asked.

"My client is suing George Anclitas for seventy-five hundred dollars. Or hadn't you heard?"

"I'd heard," the chief said noncommittally.

Fenwick pushed the chief of police slightly to one side,

77

eased an elbow over against Mason's car, smiled at the lawyer. "I'm just sort of getting oriented here, Mr. Mason. I wanted to see the lay of the land myself. Then I was going to come and have a talk with you."

"Yes?"

"That's right."

"What's your interest in me?" Mason asked.

"Well," Fenwick said, "I'm in public relations. I represent an association. George Anclitas is a member of that association."

"What's the association?" Mason asked.

Fenwick grinned. "It wouldn't mean a thing to you if I told you. It has a high-sounding name, but there's no reason for you and me to beat around the bush, Mason. The association is composed of men who are in the gambling business."

"I see," Mason said.

"You have some peculiar ideas about the law," Fenwick went on, "but because of your position, Mr. Mason, and the fact that you are a pretty shrewd lawyer, those ideas of yours could do us a lot of damage."

"They're not ideas of mine," Mason said. "They're ideas of the courts of the State of California."

"So I understand," Fenwick said.

Mason saw Della Street walk quickly to the end of the swimming pool, look across at the car, then as she was aware that the lights were not on and that two men were talking to Perry Mason, she moved around the end of the swimming pool and out of sight.

Fenwick said, "You know, this association is pretty powerful, Mr. Mason. That is, we have a lot of mighty nice people who are members, and it isn't just in this county. In fact, it isn't just in this state, although my territory is all within the state—places in Nevada, for instance, have—"

"I take it," Mason said, "you also look after the legislative interest of gambling establishments."

"Among other things," Fenwick said. "You know, Mason, a lot of people like to knock gambling; but, after all, there's nothing wrong with it. Gambling is an outlet for the emotions. All people gamble. It's universal. You can't stop it. Prisoners in penitentiaries gamble, every fraternal organization has its little gambling setup. Even the society women with their bridge clubs gamble.

"I'll tell you something else, Mason. Gambling makes good business. It puts money in circulation. It encourages sociability, and it's darned good business for a community. Now, you take right here in Rowena. You'd be surprised how much money comes into this city from gambling. People come in from all over this part of the country to do a little card playing—and they leave money here."

"I take it," Mason said, "the gamblers don't quite break even."

Fenwick threw back his head and laughed. "You're a card, Mr. Mason, you really are! Of course that's the whole principle of organized gambling, Mr. Mason. The customer doesn't break even. Hell's bells, he doesn't want to. If he wanted to break even, he'd stay home. He wouldn't go out to a gambling place at all.

"That's the real philosophy back of gambling. Sometimes the customer makes a profit. The gambler always makes a profit. Everybody knows that. The gambler isn't doing business for nothing. Some people lose and some people win. More people lose than win, but the people that win, win heavy. They sit in a game with fifty dollars and they leave it with five hundred or fifteen hundred. That's the lure. That's what keeps the wheels running.

"On the other hand, a gambler knows that while somebody may win fifteen hundred dollars in a game in the course of a week, the majority of people who sit in the game are going to contribute. That's where he makes his living, and, believe me, Mr. Mason, gambling is a good thing for a community."

"It's a matter of opinion," Mason said.

"Now, you look at this place here at Rowena," Fenwick

79

went on. "It's well policed, orderly, quiet and law abiding. You don't have any holdups here. You don't have any problems with gangsters. The place just runs along smoothly, and people like George Anclitas are heavy taxpayers—I mean really heavy taxpayers."

"You mean gambling is a good thing for the community," Mason said, "for the citizens who make up the community?"

"That's right. Now you're getting the idea."

"Then there's no reason why we shouldn't tell the married women that the husband has the management of community property but he can't gamble it away. If a gambler wins the wife's share of community property, he can't keep it."

The smile faded from Fenwick's face. "Now *that's* a horse of another color, Mason. You're getting things all mixed up. I didn't say that, and we don't feel that way.

"In the first place, I think that when you make a careful study of the law you'll find you're mistaken, and frankly I'd like to have you make a careful study of the law. That's going to take some time, Mr. Mason. You're a lawyer, and we don't want you to do it for nothing. My association needs some representation here, and we'd like to retain you to sort of keep us advised on the law.

"One of the first things we'd like to have you do would be to take a year or so and really study up on the decisions relating to gambling and games of chance. We'd put you under a retainer of, say, fifteen thousand a year."

Mason grinned. "What do you want *me* for, Fenwick? You've already hired Gowrie."

Fenwick's eyes widened. "How did you know?" he asked. Mason grinned.

"Well," Fenwick said, "after all, Mason, we're both of us grown up. Think this proposition over, will you?"

Mason shook his head. "I'm busy with trial work," he said. "I don't have many interests outside of that."

"Well, you sure knew some law that threw a monkey wrench in the machinery of *our* organization," Fenwick said.

80

"Boy, they got me on the telephone and told me to get down here so fast it'd make your head swim. I was on a vacation down at Acapulco and had a very pleasant, understanding little companion along with me. Wham! Boy, did I get a telephone call! Get on the plane, get up to Rowena, talk with George Anclitas, talk with Perry Mason, talk with Darwin Gowrie, talk with Mrs. Helman Ellis!"

"You evidently made good time," Mason said.

"I made good time. I can get along without sleep when I have to and still keep going."

Fenwick hesitated for a moment, then met Mason's eyes. "Well, why not?" he asked. "Sure, I've seen Gowrie."

"And what about Mrs. Ellis?"

"I'm looking for her," Fenwick said. "That's why I'm still hanging around here. We can't find her. She is in some kind of a ruckus with her husband. She was away for a while. Her husband thinks she was in Arizona. But she came back early this morning, then got in the family yacht and sailed off somewhere."

"Where?" Mason asked.

"I wish I knew. I'm figuring Ensenada on a guess. I've got men covering Ensenada and Catalina. The minute her boat shows up, I'll take a plane and go talk to her. I was going to ring you up at your office and make an appointment. Finding you here has saved me a lot of trouble."

"I understood Mrs. Ellis was looking around in Arizona," Mason said.

"That's where she was. She didn't stay long. The party she was looking for wasn't where she expected to find her. She got a hot tip from some place and came back here, all worked up. She thought she'd been deliberately sent on a wild-goose chase."

"Who tipped her off?" Mason asked.

"I don't know. I heard about it, that's all, just the sort of gossip a man can pick up."

Mason stretched and yawned.

"Look here," Fenwick said, "I'm not an attorney, Mr.

81

Mason, and I'm not in a position to question your judgment about the law, but if—now, I'm just saying *if*—that decision you mentioned is out of line with the law generally or if there's been a rehearing, or if the case hasn't been decided by the State Supreme Court and this represents just an outstanding departure from the ordinary doctrine of law, I know you'd want to be the first to find out about it.

"Now, I'll tell you that we've got a battery of high-priced lawyers looking into this thing and we'll know the answer within a day or two. If, of course, your ideas about the law are wrong, you'd want to be the first one to correct the erroneous impression you gave Mrs. Ellis.

"Now, as I told you, we're willing to pay for research. We don't want you to start looking this point up for nothing. In fact, I'm authorized to give you fifteen thousand dollars just to start looking it up."

There was silence for a moment.

"In cash," Fenwick said.

"I heard you the first time," Mason said. "Right at the moment I'm busy. I won't be able to do any research work."

Fenwick extended his pudgy hand. "Well, you know where I stand, Mason. Think it over—but if you're too busy to research the point, my associates here in Rowena certainly wouldn't want to do anything that would interrupt your schedule."

"In other words," Mason said, "if I'm so damned busy, why don't I stay in my office and mind my own business."

"Something like that." Fenwick grinned, gripping Mason's hand.

The chief of police touched two fingers of his right hand to the brim of his cap, turned back toward the police car. Fenwick walked back and joined him. The car purred into motion, glided past Mason's automobile and turned to the left down the block.

Mason turned on his lights.

Della Street came out to stand by the edge of the swimming pool.

Mason started his car, drove out of the alley, across the street and swung in close to the curb.

Della Street, moving rapidly, walked across to the car, jerked the door open and jumped in.

"Everything okay?" he asked.

"Everything okay," she said. "There was one other woman in the place. When she had the attendant occupied, I went to work. There was a washbowl with open plumbing, and I got the tube of ice suspended from the two shut-off valves just as you suggested. The gun's out of sight unless someone should happen to get down on the floor and look up."

"Okay," Mason said, "we'll be on our way."

"I see that you had company."

"The chief of police and a lobbyist for the gambling interests," Mason said.

"What do the gambling interests want?"

"To retain me," Mason said. "They think I'm working too hard. They'd like to pay our expenses to Acapulco and have us keep out of circulation for a while."

"And you told them?" Della Street asked.

"That I was busy," Mason said.

"And so, now?" she asked.

"Now," Mason said, "we get out of Rowena—fast."

Chapter 8

Thursday afternoon, while Della Street was out of the office on an errand, the unlisted telephone in Mason's office buzzed its signal.

Mason, knowing that Paul Drake was the only outsider in possession of the unlisted number, dropped the book he was reading, picked up the telephone, said, "Hello. What is it?"

Paul Drake's voice, clipped with urgency, came over the phone. "Perry, have you heard from your client in that Rowena case?"

"Ellen Robb?"

"Yes."

"I haven't heard from her all day, Paul. Why?"

"Better get her," Drake said.

"What's happened?"

"I don't know for sure. I can give you some of it."

"Shoot."

"Mrs. Ellis boarded her yacht and took off for destinations unknown."

"I know," Mason said. "I talked with the lobbyist for the gambling interests, and he had an all-points bulletin out for the yacht. He thought it was due in Ensenada or in Catalina."

"Well, here's the thing," Drake said. "Sometime late this morning a submarine that was quite a ways out beyond Catalina Island noticed a boat in proscribed waters. It was drifting aimlessly. The submarine hailed the boat, got no answer and went aboard. The boarding officer found the cabin was locked, found the tanks were out of gas, that no one seemed to be aboard. He forced the cabin door and right away knew something had happened."

"Such as what?"

"Murder."

"Go on," Mason said.

"The body inside had been there for a while. It was the body of Mrs. Ellis. She had evidently tried to protect herself. There were evidences of a struggle. The gun that she had evidently tried to use was lying by her hand. One shot had been fired from it. The gun was cocked, ready for a second shot, which Mrs. Ellis never got a chance to fire. There were two bullet wounds in the body, apparently both of them chest wounds. Either one would have been fatal within a matter of minutes. There had been a massive hemorrhage, and the inside of the cabin was a mess.

"Now then, there's something that links Ellen Robb to the case. I don't know what it is, but I understand the police are looking for her. They have out an all-points bulletin and they're really making a search."

"Anything else?" Mason asked.

"That's all."

"Okay," Mason said. "I'll get busy. Where are you now?"

"At the office."

"Stay there," Mason said. "Hold a couple of good men in readiness. Now, you have bodyguards watching Ellen Robb's motel?"

"That's right."

"You've had a recent report from them?"

"Within an hour. She's at the motel."

"Any visitors?"

"Apparently she's been pure as the driven snow, if you mean has she been entertaining Helman Ellis in the motel."

"That's what I meant primarily," Mason said. "Anything else?"

"Nothing else."

Mason said, "I'm going down there, Paul, and you'd better pull your men off the job. When the police show up, if

85

they find private detectives on guard, they'll start asking questions. We may not want to answer those questions."

"Okay," Drake said. "I'll get busy."

Mason called the receptionist on the intercom, said, "When Della comes in tell her to wait for a call from me, Gertie. I'm going out on an emergency. Cancel any appointments for the next hour and a half."

He picked up his brief case, grabbed his hat, left the office and drove to the Surf and Sea Motel at Costa Mesa. He tapped on the door of Unit 19.

"Who is it?" Ellen Robb's voice asked.

"Mason," the lawyer said.

"Oh," she said. Then, after a moment, "I'm not even decent, Mr. Mason."

"Get decent," Mason said. "This is important."

"How important?" she asked, sudden alarm in her voice.

"Important enough to get me down here," Mason said.

Ellen Robb turned the key in the lock. "Come on in," she said.

Mason entered.

"Don't mind me," Ellen Robb said. "I can stand it if you can. Did you bring the papers for me to sign?"

"I brought the papers," Mason said. "I want you do to two things."

"What?"

"Sign this complaint and get some clothes on."

"Which first?"

"The complaint."

She seated herself on the stool at the dressing table, took the papers that Mason handed her, said, "Is it all right for me to sign?"

"It is," Mason said. "You're suing George and Marcus for seven thousand, five hundred dollars. Sign now, then dress, and after you dress read the complaint carefully."

She signed, then pushed back the stool.

"Want to talk to me while I dress?"

Mason hesitated a moment, then said, "It's better you

don't know what this is all about," he said. "Just get dressed. Now, remember, if anything happens before we leave here, I simply came here to have you sign these papers."

She regarded him with a puzzled expression as she carefully smoothed stockings up on her long legs, pulled a dress over her head.

"You're a deep one," she said.

Mason said, "Ellen, I want to know one thing. I want you to tell me the truth."

"What is it?"

"Were you cutting corners with Helman Ellis?"

"Why?"

"George Anclitas says you were. His partner, Slim Marcus, says you were."

"Slim!" she blazed. "He's a great one. That guy was making passes at me from the moment I came on the job, pulling the kind of stuff on me that the way to get ahead was to co-operate with the people who could help me and—"

"Never mind that," Mason said. "I'm talking about Ellis."

"Ellis," she said, "I think was . . . well, fascinated."

"How about you?" Mason asked. "Did you give him a tumble?"

"I strung him along a little bit. I was supposed to. I—"

Knuckles sounded on the door.

She looked at Mason in surprise, then called, "Who is it?"

"Police," Lt. Tragg's voice said. "Will you open up, please? We want to ask you some questions."

"This is it," Mason said.

She hurriedly buttoned her blouse.

Mason walked to the door, opened it and said, "Why, how are you, Lieutenant?"

"You!" Tragg said.

"Whom did you expect?"

Tragg took a deep breath. "I *should* have expected you. Where's Ellen Robb?"

"I'm Ellen Robb. What's the trouble?"

Ellen Robb stepped forward.

Tragg sized her up. "You know Helman Ellis of Rowena?" he asked.

"Yes. Why?"

"His wife, Nadine?"

"Yes."

"Any trouble with Nadine?"

"Now, wait a minute," Mason said. "Before you start throwing a lot of questions at my client, let's find out what it's all about."

"That's a good one," Tragg said. "No idea what it's all about, eh? What are *you* doing *here* if you don't know what it's all about?"

Mason said, "I am suing George Anclitas and his partners for claims which Miss Robb has against George for giving her a black eye, for kicking her out of her room and into the cruel, cold world when she was garbed only in her professional working attire, consisting of little more than a pair of tights and a look of extreme innocence.

"In case you want all of the details, I have just had the papers prepared in my office and I came here to get Miss Robb to sign them."

"We'll look around," Tragg said.

"Got a warrant?"

"That's right. Here it is."

"What are you looking for?" Mason asked.

"A murder weapon, in case you didn't know."

"Who's dead?" Mason asked.

Tragg smiled and shook his head.

"Now, you look here," Ellen Robb said, "you can't pin—"

"Shut up, Ellen," Mason said. "I'll do *all* the talking."

"That's what you think," Tragg told him. "You're leaving."

"Not until you've finished with the search," Mason said.

"Look around," Tragg told a plain-clothes man who was with him.

Tragg seated himself on the bed, looked from Mason to Ellen Robb. "It certainly is lucky finding you here. Let's take a look at those papers you say she just signed."

Mason opened his brief case, took out the signed copies, said, "Here you are, Lieutenant."

Lt. Tragg carefully inspected the signature of Ellen Robb. "It *looks* as though she had just signed it," he said. "Perhaps she did. I—"

"Lieutenant," the plain-clothes man said.

Tragg turned.

"This way," the plain-clothes man said.

Tragg stood, peering down at the revolver that had been uncovered in the suitcase.

"Well, well, well! What's this?" he asked.

"I don't know," Ellen Robb said. "It's a revolver that I found in my baggage when I left George Anclitas' place— you know, The Big Barn in Rowena."

"And when was that?"

"I left Tuesday night."

"And you noticed this in your things this morning?"

"Yes."

"And what did you do about it?"

"Let's not answer any questions about that gun right now," Mason said. "Let's wait until we know why Lieutenant Tragg is interested in the gun."

"I'm interested in it," Tragg said, "because it's a .38-caliber Smith & Wesson revolver, and I want to know about it."

"My client found it in her baggage," Mason said. "She told me about it as soon as she discovered it. I advised her to leave it there."

"She didn't know anything at all about it, about where it came from or anything about it? It isn't her gun?"

"That's right. She just found it there. Someone evidently put that gun in her suitcase."

"How nice," Lt. Tragg said sarcastically. "How perfectly nice that Ellen Robb has an attorney representing her. What a happy coincidence that you were here."

"What's so important about the gun?" Mason asked.

"We'll tell you about that a little later," Tragg said.

"Well, let me give you a little advice," Mason told him. "Just so you don't stick your neck out too far, Tragg, don't make any statements about that gun until you know what you're talking about."

"What do you mean?"

"I think you'll find that gun has absolutely no significance whatever."

"What do you mean, no significance whatever?"

"Just what I said. I can't elaborate. I'm giving you a personal, friendly tip, Lieutenant."

"Thanks," Tragg said. "I could hardly hold down my job if it wasn't for your personal, friendly tips, Perry."

"This one may be a little more significant than you think at the moment."

"Why? What do you know?"

"Not very much as yet," Mason said. "But there is a chance I may know more than my client."

"Should you hold out on her that way?" Tragg asked sarcastically.

"It may be for the best interests of all concerned," Mason said.

Tragg said, "Miss Robb, would you mind letting me take your fingerprints so I can make a comparison with certain photographs?"

Ellen Robb looked questioningly at Perry Mason.

"Let him take your fingerprints," Mason said.

Tragg opened the bag he was carrying, took out a portable fingerprint outfit, took Ellen Robb's fingerprints, then studied them carefully with a magnifying glass.

He looked up at Ellen Robb, said, "You knew that Helman Ellis had a yacht that he called *Cap's Eyes*?"

She nodded.

"You've been aboard that yacht?"

"Yes."

"When was the last time?"

"Early Tuesday evening."

"What time?"

"I don't know. About . . . oh, I'd say along about dusk."

"What were you doing aboard?"

"Looking for Mrs. Ellis."

"Did you find her?"

"No one was aboard. I heard that she and her husband were going on a cruise. I wanted to catch her before they left."

"Why were you so anxious to see her?"

"I wanted to talk with her."

"What about?"

"About various things. About . . . well, frankly, because I wanted to discuss her husband with her."

"Why should you be discussing her husband with her?"

"I think she had become jealous of me."

"Why?"

"I worked at The Big Barn, and her husband, Helman, spent some time there."

"And you talked with him?"

"At The Barn?"

"Yes."

"Of course I talked with him. That was part of my job, to keep the customers feeling good."

"And Mrs. Ellis resented that?"

"Frankly, I don't know. I heard she was jealous and I wanted to see her."

"Why?"

"I wanted to tell her there was absolutely no ground for any jealousy whatever."

"So you went aboard the yacht?"

"Yes."

"And you had this gun with you?"

"No."

"No?"

"No. Definitely not. That was before the gun was put in my bag."

"How do you know?"

"Well, I . . . well, I'll say this. That was before I discovered the gun in my bag."

"That's better. You don't know when it was put there?"

"Not definitely, no."

"And you left The Big Barn that night?"

"Later on, yes."

"And you didn't see Mrs. Ellis on the yacht?"

"No."

"Did you see Mr. Ellis that night?"

"I saw him later, shortly before the trouble with George Anclitas."

"Did you tell him you were looking for his wife?"

"He told me his wife had been looking for me, and I told him that there was absolutely no reason for her to be jealous, at least as far as I was concerned."

"And what did Helman tell you?"

"He said his wife got these unreasoning spells of jealousy, and when she did, that you couldn't reason with her or anything. He said that he had been planning on going on a cruise with her but that she'd taken the skiff and gone ashore and left him marooned on the boat."

"And when was that?"

"That was Tuesday night."

"Did you also talk with him last night?"

"Now, just a minute," Mason said. "I think this questioning has gone far enough, Lieutenant."

"Okay," Lt. Tragg said rather cheerfully. "I just want to ask Miss Robb one question. Did you at any time ever enter the cabin of Ellis' yacht, the *Cap's Eyes*?"

"At any time?"

"At any time."

"No."

"You knew the yacht?"

"Yes."

"You'd been aboard it?"

"Well . . . yes, I went aboard once with Helman, when he was showing me around."

"Did you go in the cabin then?"

"I . . . I may have."

"When was that?"

"Oh, some time ago."

"How long ago?"

"Two weeks ago."

"Did you kill Nadine Ellis while you were on that yacht?"

"Did I kill Nadine Ellis? *What* are you talking about?"

"I'm talking about murder," Tragg said. "Did you see her Wednesday and kill her?"

"Good heavens no! I didn't—Why? Is she—You mean she's been—?"

Mason said, "Now, I'm going to give you some instructions, Ellen. Don't answer any more questions. You have given Lieutenant Tragg a very fair, straight and direct statement. There is no reason for Lieutenant Tragg to browbeat you, bully you, cross-examine you or try to give you a third-degree. If, however, Lieutenant Tragg wants you to accompany him, do so. But don't make *any* statement under *any* circumstances. Don't say one more word about this case or about your relations with George Anclitas, about the suit that I'm going to file or about anything, unless I am present and instruct you to make a statement."

"All right, Mason," Tragg said. "You've spoken your piece. You can leave now. There was a chance we might have been able to get an explanation which would have prevented a lot of notoriety for Miss Robb. But in view of your instructions to her, she's going to have to come to Headquarters."

"That's fine," Mason said. "She'll go to Headquarters—How long are you going to hold her there?"

"Probably until we can have some test bullets fired from this gun," Tragg said, "and have the test bullets compared by the ballistics department with the fatal bullets which killed Mrs. Ellis."

"Go right ahead," Mason said. "Accompany him, Miss Robb. Make no statement to newspaper reporters. Don't talk to anyone. Simply clam up and keep quiet. You've made your statement. Now then, when Lieutenant Tragg tells you that you can leave, get in touch with me at once."

"You mean *if*," Tragg said, "not *when*."

Mason grinned. "Once more, Lieutenant, you have failed to understand me. I mean *when*. I said *when* and I meant *when*."

Chapter 9

Mason, pacing the floor of his office, made comments from time to time to an attentive Della Street.

Della, knowing that the lawyer was simply thinking out loud, used her knowledge of his character to facilitate the thought processes. At times she would nod her head, at times listen with rapt attention, and at times interpose some shrewd question.

Mason, pacing back and forth, said, "That probably explains why they didn't make any commotion about the gun."

"Who?" Della Street asked.

"George Anclitas," Mason said. "He was framing a crime on Ellen Robb, all right, but it wasn't anything simple like the crime of stealing a gun."

"Then he must have known a murder had been committed?"

"Yes."

"How would he have known that?"

"There's only one way," Mason said. "He must have killed her. He must have killed her with that gun and then planted that gun in Ellen Robb's suitcase."

"Then Mrs. Ellis was killed before the gun ever came into Ellen's possession?"

"That has to be it," Mason said, and resumed pacing the floor.

After a moment Della Street ventured an inquiry. "Where does that leave us?" she asked.

Mason stopped abruptly in his pacing, snapped his fingers and said, "Damn!"

Della Street raised her eyebrows.

"I hadn't thought of it from that angle," Mason said. "I've been too busy trying to unscramble what must have happened in connection with the murder so I could protect my client's interests."

"You're thinking of it from that angle now?" Della Street asked.

"I'm thinking of it from that angle now," Mason said, "and I don't like what I'm thinking."

"Why?"

"As long as the gun was simply an article of stolen property, we had every right in the world to restore it to its rightful owner and we could do that by returning it to his place of business, but if that gun becomes a valuable piece of evidence . . ."

Mason broke off and resumed pacing the floor, his eyes level-lidded with concentration.

"Isn't it our duty to report any evidence to the police?" Della Street asked.

Mason nodded, then said tersely, "It's also our duty to protect our client."

"But if the evidence came into her possession *after* the crime had been committed . . ."

"Suppose they don't believe that, Della?"

"Then, of course . . ." It was Della Street's turn to break off in the middle of a sentence and start thinking.

"Exactly," Mason said. "It puts us in the devil of a predicament."

"Can I take the sole responsibility?" Della Street asked. "After all, I was the one who took the gun back."

"You were acting under my orders," Mason said. "Don't be silly. I was taking the responsibility, and if there's any responsibility I take it all—*all*, you understand?"

"The facts," she said, "speak for themselves. I took the gun back."

Mason said, "I take the responsibility. Now, just remember that. Don't try to get yourself involved in this thing out of a sense of loyalty. Hang it! The trouble is I don't know . . . suppose she *isn't* telling the truth?''

"Who?"

"Our client," Mason said.

"She could be lying?" Della asked.

"Of course she could be lying," Mason said. "And she's just the type who would lie. She's a young woman who has sharpened her wits against the seamy side of life. She knows her way around and she's doubtless learned that everyone must look out for himself. That's the code of the society in which she's been living."

Della Street said, "Then she would have stolen the gun from The Big Barn, gone aboard the yacht, only instead of not finding anybody aboard, she had a session with Nadine Ellis and killed her. Then she came here and handed you the gun, telling you her story about having found it in her baggage."

"That's right," Mason said.

"And at that very time Mrs. Ellis must have been lying dead on the yacht."

"In that case," Mason asked, "how did the yacht get out there beyond Catalina Island?"

Della Street gave his question thoughtful consideration. "The yacht was safely moored in the harbor after you switched guns?"

Mason grinned. "It must have been," he said, "and that fact is going to give Hamilton Burger, the district attorney, and Lieutenant Arthur Tragg of Homicide, a terrific jolt. That fact, Della, puts our client in the clear and puts us in the clear."

"Just how will the D.A.'s office get jolted?" Della Street asked.

"Finding a gun in Ellen Robb's possession, thinking that it's the murder weapon, getting everything all built up, turning the fatal bullets over to the ballistics department and then finding that they didn't come from that gun at all."

"In that event, what gun did they come from?" Della Street asked.

Mason stroked the angle of his jaw with the tips of his fingers. "I wish I knew the answer to that," he said. "It doesn't seem possible that the bullets could have come from the gun that we returned to The Big Barn . . . but if they did . . . *if* they did, we're in one hell of a predicament, Della."

"What would we have to do?"

"I'm darned if I know," Mason said. "If I keep quiet I'm perhaps compounding a felony, perhaps making myself an accessory after the fact—to use a legal expression—in a murder case."

"And if you go to the police and tell them the story?"

"If I go to the police and tell them the story," Mason said, "they won't believe me. They'll think I am simply trying to work some elaborate scheme to trap the police and throw the prosecution off the track. And in any event I'd still be in a jam, this time for betraying the interests of a client."

"Are you honor bound to keep all the facts in connection with her case confidential?"

"Probably not," Mason said. "Strictly speaking, a privileged communication is rather limited. A lawyer is technically only entitled to protect the confidences of his client within a very limited field. The confidences are those that are given to the attorney in order to enable him to represent the interests of his client.

"That's the narrow, technical rule. Practically, by both usage and custom, the rule has been expanded. I know as far as *I'm* concerned, I'd rather have my hand cut off than betray the interests of a client. If I'm representing a client, I want the representation to be honest, loyal and efficient. I make it a point to believe everything my client tells me and to act accordingly in order to protect the best interests of that client."

"Yet you recognize there's a possibility the client may lie?"

"I recognize the possibility the client may lie," Mason said.

"Well," Della Street said, "as I see it, there's nothing to be done until the police get a report from the ballistics department on those bullets."

"That's right," Mason said. "*After* they find out that the bullets that killed Mrs. Ellis didn't come from that gun, then the question is, did they come from the gun we took from Ellen Robb? If they didn't, we're in the clear. If they did, then we're right slap-bang behind the eight ball."

"We can find out?" Della Street asked.

"We can find out," Mason said, "because fortunately I had Paul Drake get a ballistics expert to fire test bullets from the gun. We have those test bullets. Paul Drake can get photographs of the fatal bullets, and we can compare the striations. That's not the best way of making a comparison, but it will do under the circumstances. We can reach a pretty fair opinion. In other words, if the test bullets don't match the fatal bullets, we can tell. If they do, we can't be *absolutely* certain. But if we get enough lines of striation in the photograph, we'll know that there's a very good possibility the fatal bullets were fired from that gun."

"And then?" Della Street asked.

"Then we'll cross that bridge," Mason said. "We should be hearing from Paul any—"

Drake's code knock sounded on the door. Mason nodded to Della Street, who opened the door and let Paul Drake in.

Mason, standing in the middle of the office floor where he had paused mid-stride when Drake knocked on the door, nodded to the detective, said, "What's new, Paul?"

"I hate to bring bad news," Drake said, "but if the ballistics check shows that Nadine Ellis was killed by a bullet from the gun that the police took from Ellen Robb's motel room, she doesn't stand the faintest whisper of a chance."

"And if the bullets don't check?" Mason asked.

"They've probably got a case against her," Drake said, "but it won't be dead open-and-shut."

"I don't see what evidence they have," Mason said, frowning.

"Well, naturally they're not telling," Drake said. "From what I can pick up in the way of scuttle butt around Headquarters, they seem to feel they have an airtight case—and, of course, once the ballistics experts show Nadine Ellis was killed by a bullet from that gun the police took from Ellen's motel, they have a case that neither you nor any other lawyer can win. That ballistics evidence will make it a copper-riveted cinch."

"All right, Paul," Mason said. "I've got some confidential information for you. The gun won't check. Now, start working on the case from that angle and see what your investigation shows up."

"You mean the bullets weren't fired from that gun?"

"They weren't fired from that gun."

"How sure are you, Perry?"

"Positive."

"That's going to make a difference," Drake said. "But, look, Perry, you *can't* be positive. You never know when a client is lying to you and when she's telling the truth. Particularly a girl like Ellen Robb. She can be convincing as a liar. She's a past master at pulling the wool over your eyes."

Mason said, "Nobody's pulling the wool over my eyes, Paul. The bullets won't check."

"Well, that's something," Drake said. "There's one thing certain. If they don't check, that will hit the district attorney an awful wallop right between the eyes."

"He's going to be hit a wallop, then."

Drake was thoughtful. "There's only *one* way you could be certain, Perry."

"How's that, Paul?"

"That gun you gave me to take to Maurice Halstead, Perry."

"What about it?" the lawyer asked.

Drake was thoughtfully silent.

"Well?" Mason prompted.

"Look, Perry," the detective said, "if you pulled one of those gun-switching acts of yours, and if that gun I gave Halstead should prove to be the murder weapon . . . well, I'm bailing out, that's all. I can't go that far."

"No one's asked you to, Paul."

"I'd have to tell what I know."

"When?"

"As soon as I knew it made any difference in the case."

"We'll let it stand that way," Mason said.

"I'm not going to sleep tonight, Perry," Drake said.

"Take a pill."

"That won't help. Good Lord, Perry, do you know what you're doing?"

"It's not what I'm doing that worries me," Mason said. "It's what I have done."

"So what do I do now, Perry?"

"Wait until you're certain," Mason said.

"Maurice Halstead will also be doing some thinking as soon as he's seen the papers," Drake pointed out.

"Let him think, Paul," Mason said.

The phone rang.

Della Street picked up the telephone, said, "Yes," then to Paul, "It's for you, Paul."

"That'll be a report on what ballistics found out," Drake said. "I told my office to call me here if they got that report but not to bother me otherwise."

Drake picked up the telephone, said, "Hello . . . uh-huh . . . They're sure? No chance of a mistake . . . well, *that's* interesting. . . . Okay, I'll be back in the office in a few minutes. 'Bye now."

Drake hung up the telephone, cocked a quizzical eyebrow at Mason, and said, "Why were you so damned sure those bullets weren't going to match, Perry?"

The lawyer grinned. "Call me clairvoyant or psychic, Paul."

"Well," Drake said, "you'd better throw away your crystal ball and try tea leaves. The fatal bullets that killed Nadine Ellis were fired from the gun that Ellen Robb had in her possession when the police arrested her.''

Chapter 10

Donovan Fraser, a relatively new and somewhat eager-beaver deputy district attorney, arose to address the Court.

"If the Court please, we expect to show that the defendant in this case, Ellen Robb, was attempting to break up the home of the decedent, Nadine Ellis, that quite understandably friction developed between the two women, that the defendant surreptitiously and with malice aforethought entered the yacht belonging to Mr. and Mrs. Ellis, knowing that Mrs. Ellis was aboard, that she fired two shots into the body of Mrs. Ellis and then, having assured herself that her enemy was dead, she pointed the yacht out to sea, started the motors and trusted that the natural risks incident to marine navigation in a small boat of this sort would result in the loss of the boat and its grisly occupant.

"We expect to show that a gun found in the possession of the defendant, Ellen Robb, inflicted the fatal wounds upon Nadine Ellis and we shall ask that the defendant be bound over to the Superior Court for trial."

Judge Staunton Keyser looked down at the young man thoughtfully, said, "You don't need to make an opening argument to the Court in a preliminary hearing, Mr. Deputy District Attorney. As I understand it, this is simply a question of showing that a crime has been committed and that there is probable cause to believe the defendant committed that crime."

"I understand, Your Honor," Fraser said, "but in view of the well-known tactics of defense counsel, who always tries to put on a case at the time of the preliminary examination, I felt that the Court should be advised of what we are trying to do.''

''You go right ahead,'' Judge Keyser said, ''and never mind the tactics of opposing counsel. Just put on your proof. Call your first witness.''

Fraser called the captain of a Coast Guard cutter to the stand.

''Are you familiar with a yacht called *Cap's Eyes*?''

''I am.''

''Are you familiar with the documents of registration in the Coast Guard records as to ownership of that yacht?''

''Yes, sir.''

''Who owns that yacht?''

''Helman Ellis.''

''Did you have occasion to see that yacht on Thursday, the eleventh day of this month?''

''I did. Yes, sir.''

''Will you explain the circumstances.''

''We were notified by the Navy that the yacht was drifting helplessly with a murdered woman aboard. I called the FBI and the coroner's office. I was instructed to take Dr. Andover Calvert out to the yacht, together with a representative of the sheriff's office and an agent of the FBI. We had to wait a short time until these men arrived. Then we flew to Catalina, picked up a deep-sea patrol boat there and proceeded at high speed to where the yacht was located. At that time we made an inspection of the yacht. Do you want me to tell you what we found?''

''In general terms, yes.''

''The fuel tank of the yacht was quite dry. The yacht was drifting in an area which is devoted to naval maneuvers and where small craft are forbidden to venture. The body of a woman was lying in the cabin. We took photographs of the body.''

''Do you have those photographs?''

''I do.''

''We'd like to have them introduced in evidence.''

104

"No objection," Mason said.

"Very well," Judge Keyser ruled, "they may go into evidence as People's Exhibit—How many are there, Counselor?"

"Seven."

"All right, People's Exhibits A-1, A-2, A-3, A-4, A-5, A-6 and A-7. Proceed."

"What did you do?"

"After completing inspection of the yacht we fastened a tow cable and brought the yacht into port."

"Cross-examine," Fraser said.

Mason arose and approached the witness. "How long have you been with the Coast Guard, Captain?"

"Some twenty years."

"You are quite familiar with the waters around Southern California?"

"I am, yes."

"The waters where the yacht was found?"

"I am not familiar with those waters except in a general way. Most of our work is done a lot closer to the shore line."

"I understand. But you know generally the waters, and quite particularly you are familiar with the waters between the coast line and the place where the yacht was found?"

"Yes, sir."

"That yacht was some distance on the other side of Catalina Island?"

"Yes, sir."

"Now, then," Mason said, "what are the chances that the yacht with no one aboard except the dead woman could have started out from Los Angeles yacht harbor or the Deep Sea Cruising Yacht Club near Long Beach with the steering mechanism locked in position so that it would have gone in a straight line and have sailed out to the place where it was found without mishap—and without attracting attention because of failure to follow regulations or display running lights—assuming, Captain, that there was no one aboard the yacht other than the body of the decedent?"

"Ordinarily I would have said the chances would be pretty slim," the captain admitted, "but here we are confronted with an established fact. Regardless of the percentage of chances, the yacht did do that very thing."

"Now, just a moment, Your Honor," Fraser said. "I don't see the purpose of this examination. I don't see what counsel expects to accomplish by it."

"It's legitimate cross-examination," Judge Keyser said. "Anyway, the question has been answered. Let the answer stand."

"What was the cruising radius of the yacht? With a full tank of gasoline, how far would it have gone?"

"We don't know the tank was full," Fraser objected.

"This is simply cross-examination," Judge Keyser said. "He can ask anything he wants to about the yacht. The Court, frankly, is interested in this. It's rather a significant phase of the case. At least, it seems so to the Court."

"The cruising radius would have varied depending upon wind, tide and weather conditions, but if the tanks had all been full, the cruising radius would have been . . . well, somewhat beyond the point where we found the yacht."

"You're assuming, then, that the tanks were not full when the yacht was started on its journey. Is that right?"

"Yes."

"There was some sort of a steering mechanism on the yacht which would hold it to its course?"

"That is right. There are several variations of mechanical devices which hold a yacht on course. Some of them are quite elaborate, working with compass directions so that a yacht can be set on a compass course and will hold that course. Some of them are simply devices to hold the yacht steady after the course has been manually selected."

"Assuming that you were on that yacht at Long Beach, that you wanted to point it in the direction where it was located by the Navy and picked up by you, would it have been possible for you to have set that steering gear so that

106

the yacht would have been pointed in that direction and gone on until the fuel tanks became dry?''

''I think it *could* have been done, because I know it *was* done.''

''If the yacht had started from its regular mooring, wouldn't it have had to sail right through Catalina Island to arrive at the place where it was found?''

''Not necessarily.''

''What do you mean by that?''

''I think it might have been difficult, although not impossible, for the yacht to have been sailing blind through all the ocean traffic without being noticed. It *could* have cleared the westerly end of the island, then, after the fuel was exhausted, drifted to the portion of the ocean where it was found.''

''You think the yacht did that?''

''I feel certain it must have.''

''Then you feel the murderer was not aboard after the yacht left its mooring?''

''Not unless he was an exceptional swimmer.''

Judge Keyser frowned at the titter of the audience.

''What are the chances that the yacht could have made the trip without collision, without having wind and tidal currents get it off course so that it would have run into trouble?''

''That depends on what you mean by trouble. Once the course had been set so as to miss Catalina Island, there was very little to stop it.''

''Except the normal small-boat traffic on the water?''

''Yes.''

''That is a considerable factor?''

''That depends. It depends on *when* the yacht was started, it depends on conditions.''

''There were no running lights on the yacht?''

''You mean that were lit?''

''Yes.''

''No, the lights were not lit.''

''Indicating that the yacht had made its journey during daylight hours?''

"Either that or it had violated the regulations in regard to navigation."

"And if the yacht had been detected violating those regulations, something would have been done about it?"

"Yes."

"Now, this yacht was found in a restricted area?"

"Yes."

"It is customary for the Navy to use radar in that area for the purpose of detecting small boats which may have entered the area?"

"I believe so, yes."

"Therefore, if the person who started that yacht on its way had wanted the yacht to vanish, to sail on into oblivion, that person would hardly have selected that particular area?"

"Not if the individual was familiar with the restricted areas."

"And this was a restricted area?"

"Yes, sir."

"And if the person had wanted the yacht to sail on into oblivion, the fuel tanks could have been filled, and the yacht would then have gone a very considerable distance beyond the point where it was picked up, before running out of fuel?"

"Yes, sir, depending of course on whether the murderer had to accept the condition of the fuel tanks as he found them. He or she may not have dared to attempt to refuel with the body aboard—or if the murder was committed at night, there would have been little opportunity to have replenished the fuel."

"Thank you," Mason said. "That's all."

Donovan Fraser said, "Call Dr. Andover Calvert."

"I'll stipulate Dr. Calvert's qualifications, subject to the right of cross-examination," Mason said cheerfully. "Just go right ahead and ask him your technical questions."

Fraser regarded Mason with some surprise but very quickly took advantage of the opportunity. "Very well," he said. "You'll stipulate that Dr. Calvert is an examining physician connected with the office of the coroner, an autopsy surgeon, a duly qualified physician and an expert in all fields of forensic medicine?''

"Subject to the right of cross-examination," Mason said. "I'll stipulate to his general qualifications, subject to cross-examination."

"Very well. Be sworn, Dr. Calvert," Fraser instructed.

Dr. Calvert held up his right hand, was sworn, and took the witness stand.

"You boarded the yacht, the *Cap's Eyes*, on Thursday, the eleventh?''

"I did."

"That was then on the high seas?''

"Yes, sir.''

"What did you find?''

"The cabin door, which had been locked by a spring lock on the inside, had been forced open by some party before we arrived. I understand this was done by Navy personnel who had boarded the boat before the Coast Guard was notified.''

"Go on," Fraser said. "What did you find in the cabin?''

"In the cabin we found the body of a woman about twenty-eight years of age. The first stages of decomposition had set in, and I estimated the woman had been dead for somewhere between twenty-four and forty-eight hours. The woman was lying on her back on the floor of the cabin. There was an open handbag near her hand, and a cocked double-action Smith and Wesson revolver was lying near her right hand. One bullet had been discharged from this revolver and then the weapon had been cocked, apparently preparatory to firing a second shot.''

"Did you find the one bullet which had been discharged?''

"We found *a* bullet embedded in the woodwork of the cabin near the door. I believe that it was checked out by ballistics and shown to have been fired from the weapon which was lying there on the floor of the yacht near the hand of the woman.''

"You subsequently performed an autopsy on the body of this woman?''

"I did, yes, sir."

"And what did you find?"

"I found that she had been killed by gunfire. Two bullets had entered the chest cavity, slightly above and to one side of the heart. The two bullet holes were less than an inch and a half apart, and the courses of the bullets were, generally speaking, parallel."

"Had the bullets gone through the body or were they still embedded in the body?"

"One of them had been deflected and had embedded itself in bone. The other had just penetrated far enough to go through the body. It was found in the clothing of the decedent."

"These bullets were, in your opinion, the cause of death?"

"Yes."

"Cross-examine," Fraser said to Perry Mason.

Mason arose and walked toward the witness. His manner was casual and his voice was calmly conversational. "Two bullets, Doctor?"

"Yes."

"Which one inflicted the fatal wound, Doctor?"

"They both inflicted fatal wounds."

"Which one was the cause of death?"

"Either could have been the cause of death."

"Pardon me, Doctor. I'm not asking you about *could have*, I'm asking you about which *did* cause death."

"Both of them inflicted fatal wounds."

"Would you say both bullets caused death?"

"Yes."

"Would you say that a person could die twice?"

"That isn't what I mean."

"What *do* you mean?"

"I mean that either bullet might have caused death and either bullet could have caused death."

"How far apart were the bullets?"

"Around an inch and a half at the point of entrance."

"And which one was fired first?"

110

"I have no way of knowing."

"Were the bullets instantly fatal?"

"That depends on what you mean by instantly."

"Well, what do you mean by it?"

"When I say instantly I mean instantaneously."

"Did either of these wounds inflict an instantaneously fatal wound?"

"Both of the bullets instantaneously inflicted a mortal wound."

"How long after the first wound before the victim died?"

"That I don't know. It couldn't have been more than a few minutes at most."

"You think perhaps it was as much as five minutes?"

"Perhaps."

"Ten minutes?"

"Perhaps."

"Fifteen minutes?"

"I consider it very unlikely. Actually I think death occurred within a matter of two or three minutes."

"And which bullet wound caused death?"

"Oh, Your Honor," Fraser said, getting to his feet, "I object to this type of cross-examination. The questions have already been asked and answered."

"They've been asked," Mason said, "but they haven't been answered."

"Furthermore, it's incompetent, irrelevant and immaterial. It doesn't make any difference," Fraser went on.

Judge Keyser said, "I'd like to hear from counsel if he feels the questions are pertinent or relevant to any particular point."

"I think it is very important to find out how the victim died, when the victim died and what caused the death of the victim. I think that's important in any murder case," Mason said.

"But where an assailant fired two bullets, does it make any difference which bullet was fired first or which wound was the one which produced death?" Judge Keyser asked.

111

"How do *we* know that the assailant fired two bullets?" Mason asked.

Judge Keyser looked at Mason with an expression of swift surprise. "Are you contending there were two assailants?" he asked.

"Frankly, I don't know," Mason said. "I am contending at the moment, as the legal representative of this defendant, that I have the right to find out *all* the facts in the case."

"The objection is overruled," Judge Keyser said.

Dr. Calvert said angrily, "Let me make this statement to the Court and counsel. There were two bullets. One of the bullets actually penetrated a portion of the heart. I consider that bullet produced almost instantaneous death. The other bullet was a little to the left. It missed the heart but would have been fatal within a few minutes . . . that is, that's my opinion."

"All right," Mason said. "Let's call the bullet that missed the heart bullet number one and the bullet which penetrated a portion of the heart bullet number two. Which was fired first?"

"I don't know."

"I submit that it's incompetent, irrelevant and immaterial," Fraser said. "This is simply a case of an attorney trying to grasp desperately at the straw of some technicality."

Judge Keyser shook his head. "I think there is an interesting point here. I don't know what the other evidence will show, but if counsel is pursuing this lead with some definite objective in mind, it is manifestly unfair to deprive the defendant of the right of a searching cross-examination. Therefore, I will overrule the objection."

"Which bullet caused death, Doctor?"

"I don't know. It depends upon the sequence in which the bullets were fired."

"If," Mason said, "the bullet we have referred to as bullet number two was fired first and bullet number one was fired after an interval of as much as three minutes, you would

112

assume that bullet number one was fired into a dead body. Is that correct?"

"If you want to assume anything like that, I would say yes."

"If bullet number one was fired first, it would have been how long before death intervened?"

"My best opinion would be three to five minutes."

"But it could have been as much as ten minutes?"

"Yes."

"Now, suppose that after bullet number one was fired and, assuming that it was fired first, bullet number two was fired almost immediately, then death actually occurred from bullet number two."

"I would so assume if we accept those premises."

"Both bullet number one and bullet number two were recovered?"

"That's right. Both of them were taken from the body."

"And what did you do with them?"

"I personally gave them to Alexander Redfield, the ballistics expert."

"And what did you tell him when you gave him the bullets?"

"That they were the bullets taken from the body of Nadine Ellis."

"You had identified the body by that time?"

"It had been identified so that I could make that statement to Mr. Redfield."

"You gave him both bullets?"

"Yes."

"Did you mark them in any way?"

"I made a small secret mark on the bullets, yes."

"So that you can identify them?"

"Yes."

Mason said, "I assume that the prosecution has the bullets here and that they will shortly be introduced in evidence. I think that Dr. Calvert should identify the bullets at this time."

"We can identify them," Fraser said, "by having the witness Redfield testify that the bullets he produces are the ones he received from Dr. Calvert.''

"I would like to connect up every link in the chain,'' Mason said. "I think I have a right to do so.''

Fraser said angrily, "If the Court please, I was warned that I would encounter just these badgering tactics from counsel. After all, this is only a preliminary examination, and I am not going to be trapped into making a big production of it.''

"I'm not making a big production of it,'' Mason said. "I am simply asking that the witness produce the bullets that he mentioned in his testimony. He stated he recovered them from the body of Nadine Ellis. I want to see those bullets.''

"I think counsel is within his rights,'' Judge Keyser said. "Certainly you intend to produce the bullets within a few minutes, Mr. Deputy District Attorney.''

"I do,'' Fraser said, "but I want to put on my case in my own way and not have the defense attorney tell me how I'm going to do it.''

"Come, come,'' Judge Keyser said. "Apparently it doesn't make any difference. If you have the bullets here, why not produce them? Is there any reason why they can't be produced or why you are reluctant to produce them?''

"No, Your Honor.''

"Let the witness identify them, then.''

Fraser, with poor grace, turned to Alexander Redfield, the ballistics expert who was seated directly behind him, and accepted a glass test tube from Redfield. He approached the witness stand and handed this test tube to the doctor.

"I hand you two bullets, Doctor. I'll ask you to look at them and state whether or not they are the bullets you took from the body of the decedent.''

Dr. Calvert took a magnifying glass from his pocket, inspected the bullets through the glass test tube, then nodded slowly. "These are the bullets,'' he said. "They both have my secret mark on them.''

114

"What is your secret mark?" Mason asked. "Where is it?"

"I prefer to keep it secret," Dr. Calvert said. "It is a very small mark that I make and it serves to identify the bullets which I recover in the course of my autopsies."

"Then you use the same mark on all of your bullets?" Mason asked.

"That's right."

"Why?"

"So I can identify them. So that they are not to be confused with bullets that are recovered by some of the other autopsy surgeons. In that way I know my own work."

"I see," Mason said. "You use the same mark on all bullets you recover?"

"That's what I said, yes!" Dr. Calvert snapped.

"Then may I ask how many bullets you recover in the course of a year from bodies in connection with your own autopsies?"

"I don't know. It isn't a standard amount. It varies, depending on the number of autopsies, the number of homicides by shooting, and various other factors."

"Do you recover as many as fifty bullets a year?"

"Not on an average, no, sir."

"As many as twenty-five?"

"I think perhaps in some years I have recovered twenty-five. I wouldn't say that was an average."

"As many as twelve?"

"Yes, I would think so."

"And the only way you have of identifying these bullets is by your secret mark?"

"That is right. That is all the identification I need."

"It may be all the identification *you* need, Doctor, but as I understand it, these two bullets are now identified simply as being bullets which you recovered, not bullets which were recovered from the body of Nadine Ellis."

"Well, I know that those are the bullets."

"How do you know?"

"I can tell by looking at them, the shape of the bullets, the caliber."

"Then why was it necessary for you to put your secret mark on them?"

"So there would be no mistake."

"The same secret mark that you put on an average of a dozen bullets a year, that you have at times put on as many as twenty-five bullets in a year?"

"Oh, Your Honor," Fraser said. "This is argumentative. The question has been asked and answered. It's simply an attempt on the part of counsel to browbeat the witness."

Judge Keyser regarded Mason thoughtfully, then turned to the witness. "Isn't there anything that you use in the line of a label or identification on these bullets that shows they are the particular bullets that were recovered in this particular case?"

"I handed them to Alexander Redfield," Dr. Calvert said. "They were in a test tube when I handed them to him, and the test tube had a number; that is, there was a piece of paper pasted on the test tube, and that test tube had a number. It was the number of the case as it was listed in our files. If that number were on this test tube, it would definitely identify the bullets as having come from that particular body."

"But that number has been removed?" Judge Keyser asked.

"Apparently it has. I notice that the label that is on the test tube now bears the handwriting of Mr. Redfield."

"Very well," Judge Keyser said. "Go ahead and resume your inquiry, Mr. Mason. I will state to the prosecutor, however, that before these bullets can be introduced in evidence, they must be connected more directly with the particular case."

"That is what I intend to do," Fraser said, "if I am only given the chance."

"Well, you'll have every opportunity," Judge Keyser snapped. "Proceed, Mr. Mason."

"Now then," Mason said, "assuming that these bullets

116

are the bullets which you took from the body of Nadine Ellis, which bullet was fired first?''

"I've told you I don't know."

"Well, I'll put it this way," Mason said. "We referred to the bullets as bullet number one and bullet number two. Now, which of these bullets is bullet number one, as far as your testimony is concerned, and which is bullet number two?"

"I don't know."

"You don't know?"

"No."

"You didn't mark the bullets so you could distinguish them?"

"Certainly not. Both bullets came from the body. Both would have been fatal. I mean either would have been fatal. I put them in a test tube, put the code number of the case on it—which was, I believe, C-122—and personally handed the test tube to Mr. Redfield."

Redfield, who was smiling, got to his feet, started to say something, then changed his mind and sat down.

Mason said, "In other words, Doctor, the gunshot wounds in the body of Nadine Ellis showed that one wound, where the bullet actually penetrated a portion of the heart, was probably almost instantly fatal. The other inflicted a wound which would have been fatal within a few minutes. Now, you can't tell which of these bullets inflicted which wound?"

"I made no attempt to keep the bullets separate. They are both the same caliber, they were both fired from the same gun. I will state, however, that the bullet which we have referred to as bullet number two—the one which hit a portion of the heart—lodged in the spine and was somewhat flattened by the vertebra. I notice that one of these bullets is somewhat flattened, and on the strength of that I would state that in all human probability that bullet is the bullet I referred to as bullet number two—the one that hit the heart."

"Was your autopsy such that you traced each bullet as to its course?" Mason asked. "All the way through the body?"

"I traced one bullet from the point of entrance through

the heart and I traced the other bullet from the point of entrance through one of the major blood vessels. I may state, however, that I did not—or perhaps I should say that I was not able—to keep the paths of the bullets completely separate because they started to converge slightly, and the deterioration of the body due to decomposition and putrefaction was such that it was virtually impossible to segregate the course of the bullets all the way through the body.''

"And you can't tell which of these bullets was fired first?"

"That's right," Dr. Calvert said. And then suddenly added, in indignation, "And that, Mr. Mason, is because I am a man of medicine and not a medicine man."

"And," Mason went on urbanely, "you don't know for certain that these were the bullets that you took from the body of Mrs. Ellis. You only know that they were two bullets which you recovered in the course of your autopsy work."

"I took these two bullets from the body of Mrs. Ellis and handed them to Alexander Redfield on the evening of the twelfth," Dr. Calvert said.

"Thank you," Mason said. "That's all."

"No further questions," Fraser said. "You may be excused, Doctor. I'll call Alexander Redfield as my next witness."

Redfield, smiling slightly, came to the stand.

"Your name is Alexander Redfield, you are employed by the county as a ballistics expert and scientific investigator?" Fraser asked.

"That's right."

"Are you acquainted with Dr. Andover Calvert, the witness who just testified?"

"I am."

"Did you see him in this county on or about the twelfth of this month?"

"I did."

"Did you have any conversation with Dr. Calvert on that date?"

"I did."

"Did Dr. Calvert give you any objects on that date?"

"He did."

"What objects did he give you?"

"Two bullets."

"And what did you do with those two bullets, Mr. Redfield?"

"I put them in a test tube, sealed the test tube and marked the test tube for identification. Then I locked the test tube in a special compartment in the safe in my office."

"You made no comparison of the bullets with any test bullets?"

"Not at that date."

"When was that done?"

"Later, when I was given a weapon and asked to test fire that weapon."

"And what weapon was that?"

"That was a Smith and Wesson revolver with a two-and-a-half-inch barrel."

"Do you know the number of that gun?"

"I do. It was 133347."

"Do you have that gun?"

"I do."

"Will you produce it, please?"

Redfield reached in his brief case and pulled out the gun.

"I ask that this be marked for identification," Fraser said.

"It will be marked People's Exhibit B," Judge Keyser said.

"Now then, you received two bullets from Dr. Calvert. I will ask you if you have those bullets with you?"

"I just gave them to you."

"Here they are. Will you tell us whether or not those are the same bullets which Dr. Calvert gave you?"

"Those are the same bullets."

"How do you know?"

"They have been in my custody since the time Dr. Calvert handed them to me."

"And have remained in that test tube?"

"No, sir. I took them out of the test tube from time to time for the purpose of making comparisons and taking comparison photographs."

"Did the bullets ever leave your possession?"

"No, sir. They were in my possession from the time Dr. Calvert gave them to me until I handed them to you just a minute ago."

"I'll ask the bullets be marked for identification as People's Exhibit C," Fraser said.

"Both bullets as one exhibit?" Mason asked.

"They're in the test tube."

"I suggest that they be identified separately," Mason said. "I notice that one of the bullets is flattened on the nose of the bullet, evidently from hitting some rather solid object. The flattening is on a slant, and the edges of the bullet have been curled over. The other bullet shows little damage. I suggest that the flattened bullet be People's Exhibit C-1 and the other bullet be C-2. I will also state that in order to expedite matters I will stipulate that both the gun and the bullets may be received in evidence, which will obviate the necessity of marking them for identification now and introducing them into evidence later."

"Very well," Fraser said. "The People accept that stipulation. The bullets will go into evidence as People's Exhibit C-1 and People's Exhibit C-2."

Fraser turned to the witness. "Did you test-fire this gun, People's Exhibit B?"

"I did."

"And did you compare the test bullets fired from that gun with the bullets, Exhibits C?"

"Yes."

"What did you find?"

"The bullets were fired from that gun," Redfield said. "I have photographs made through a comparison microscope which shows the bullets superimposed one upon the other and the lines of striation."

"Will you produce those photographs, please?"

Redfield produced a photograph.

"I ask that this be received in evidence as People's Exhibit D."

"No objection," Mason said.

"Cross-examine," Fraser said.

Redfield, who had been cross-examined by Mason on many occasions, turned his eyes slowly and appraisingly toward the lawyer and settled himself in the witness chair. His face showed that he intended to weigh each question carefully and not be trapped into any inadvertent admission.

"There is only one photograph," Mason said, "but there are two bullets."

"The one photograph is of bullet Exhibit C-2. Since the other bullet was damaged and it would have been more difficult to have matched the striations, I didn't photograph that bullet."

"And you are completely satisfied that the bullets were fired from this gun which has been introduced in evidence as Exhibit B?"

"Yes. . . . Now, wait a minute. I don't think I made detailed tests of the damaged bullet. I did make detailed tests of the undamaged bullet and I made this photograph of it so there could be no question that it came from the gun, Exhibit B."

"You assumed that both bullets were fired from the same gun," Mason said.

"That's right."

"But you didn't check it?"

"I didn't check the damaged bullet to the same extent that I did the other."

"You checked it?"

"Well, now, just a moment, Mr. Mason. If you want to be painstakingly accurate about this, I am not in a position to swear that I did check both individual bullets. I know that I checked the undamaged bullet and I checked the damaged bullet to the extent that I determined they were both of the same caliber and weight and had been fired from a Smith and Wesson revolver. That can be told from the angle and pitch of the grooves. But as far as actual striations are concerned, I think I checked only the bullet which has been identified as Exhibit C-2.''

"Look here," Judge Keyser said, "let's be realistic about this thing, Mr. Mason. Does this point make any actual difference in the case?''

"It does not, Your Honor," Fraser fairly shouted. "It is simply another one of defense counsel's very adroit moves which he is noted for."

"May I be heard, Your Honor?" Mason asked in a quiet voice.

Judge Keyser nodded. "You may be heard. My question was addressed to you."

"I think it is a *very* important point, if the Court please," Mason said. "I think I will be in a position to prove that if a bullet from this gun was fired into the body of Nadine Ellis, the bullet *must* have been fired after Nadine Ellis was dead.

"The defendant in this case is being tried for murder. Murder is the unlawful killing of a human being with malice aforethought. If a bullet was fired from this gun into the body of Nadine Ellis *after* she was dead, the defendant certainly isn't guilty of murder. That is, the evidence relied upon to prove her guilty of murder would prove only that she had discharged a bullet into a dead body."

"That's sheer bosh and nonsense," Fraser exclaimed heatedly. "As far as this hearing is concerned, all we need to do is to prove that Nadine Ellis was murdered, that the bullets in her body came from a gun found in the possession of the defendant."

"One of the bullets," Mason said.

"That's only a matter of expediency," Fraser said. "I will admit that the prosecution would have liked it better if the ballistics expert, Alexander Redfield, had taken the time and the trouble to have identified both bullets. But since one bullet was slightly damaged and apparently they both were fired from the same gun, he contented himself with making a positive, definite identification of only one of the bullets.

"Now, since it is only incumbent upon us to show that a crime has been committed and that there is reasonable ground to believe that the defendant committed the crime, we are quite content to introduce this gun in evidence, to introduce this bullet and rest our case."

"Now, just a minute," Judge Keyser said. "Ordinarily the Court is aware of the fact that the defense doesn't put on testimony in the preliminary hearing, and if the defense does, the Court usually disregards it unless it overwhelmingly establishes the innocence of the defendant. Courts usually feel that conflicts in evidence are to be tried in the Superior Court before a jury and that where the prosecution has made a *prima-facie* case, the Court doesn't need to look any further. However, here we have a situation where a young woman, if bound over, would probably be held in jail for some time before the case came up for trial. Her reputation would be blackened, the experience would leave a psychic scar. This Court has no intention of submitting this young woman to such an ordeal simply because of technicalities.

"If Mr. Mason assures this Court that he believes he can establish the fact that this bullet could only have been fired from this gun after death had taken place, the Court certainly feels that Mr. Redfield should identify that other bullet as having come from the same gun."

"We have no objection to that," Fraser said, "except that it simply results in a delay and newspaper notoriety, both of which are greatly desired by defense counsel."

"That will do," Judge Keyser said. "There is no occasion for personalities and, after all, if you want to be technical about it, the fault, if any, rests with the prosecution. The defense is entitled to have the scientific evidence fairly examined and fairly presented. Mr. Redfield, how long will it take you to classify that somewhat damaged bullet and show that it either came from this gun, Exhibit B, or that it did not come from that weapon?"

Redfield hesitated and said, "I am working on an emergency matter at the moment. I interrupted my work there to come to court. I can promise to have the information by late this afternoon, but I am not certain that I could have it earlier."

Judge Keyser said, "I will adjourn this matter until three-thirty this afternoon. Try and have the information by that time, Mr. Redfield. If you can't possibly have it, we will continue the case until tomorrow morning. However, I would like to dispose of the case today and I think that the information concerning this bullet is of prime importance—I take it that the prosecution has evidence that this gun, Exhibit B, was found in the possession of the defendant and there can be no question of that?"

"That is right," Fraser said.

"Well, I'm going to adjourn court until three-thirty this afternoon," Judge Keyser said. "The witness will return at that time, and counsel will be present with the defendant. The defendant is remanded to custody."

Ellen Robb dug her fingers deep into Mason's coat sleeve. "Mr. Mason, how in the world—They're crazy. I didn't shoot Nadine Ellis. I never fired that gun at all. I—"

"Just sit tight," Mason said, warning her with a glance. "Don't make any statement. Newspaper reporters may try to get you to say something. The police may question you again about that gun. Sit tight, keep quiet. And whatever you do, don't lie to me."

"I'm not lying to you."

"You have been," Mason said.

She shook her head. "If that gun fired a bullet into the body of Nadine Ellis, somebody did it before the gun came into my possession and then put it in my suitcase."

Mason studied her face searchingly. She returned his gaze with level-lidded frankness. "I cross my heart and hope to die," she said.

"That," Mason told her, "*may* not be an empty expres-
124

sion. If you're lying to me, the situation may be a lot more serious than you think.''

Mason nodded to the policewoman to take Ellen Robb into her custody, and left the courtroom with Della Street.

Chapter 11

In the small private dining room of the restaurant where Perry Mason, Della Street and Paul Drake so frequently lunched during the noon recess, the trio seated themselves at the table.

"I don't see what makes this seem such a devastating surprise to you," Paul Drake said to Mason. "I told you quite a while ago this client of yours was no lily-white angel. I take it, she's been lying to you."

"It's more serious than that, Paul," Mason said.

"How do you mean?"

"I'll let you in on a secret," Mason said. "If that gun committed the murder, I personally am mixed in it."

"Mixed in what?"

"Mixed in the murder."

"*You* are!" Drake exclaimed incredulously.

"Call it an accessory after the fact or suppressing evidence or anything you want, Paul. I just don't believe that gun could possibly have been used in the killing."

"Nevertheless, it was," Drake said. "The evidence shows it."

Mason, his face granite-hard with concentration, paid no attention to Drake's words and might not have heard him.

Drake turned to Della Street and said, "I don't get it. I've seen him skate on some awfully thin legal ice, but I've never seen him like this before."

Della Street shook her head warningly, indicating that Drake was not to pursue the subject.

Drake said, "What became of the gun that you gave me

to test, Perry? That was registered in the name of George Anclitas.''

"Just don't ask questions," Mason said. "Just eat your lunch.''

The waiter brought in their orders, and Mason ate in thoughtful silence.

"Well," Drake said, as he pushed back his plate, "thanks for the lunch, Perry. I *have* had more cheerful meals.''

Mason merely grunted in acknowledgment of Drake's remark.

"I'll get the chores done," Drake said, and left the dining room.

Della Street glanced solicitously at Perry Mason, started to say something, then checked herself.

As though reading her mind, Mason said, "I know you're wondering what's worrying me. The thing that worries me is whether the district attorney's office has baited an elaborate trap for me and I'm walking into it, or whether they have considered the case so dead open-and-shut they don't need to worry."

Della Street shook her head. "Hamilton Burger has his faults, but he's not entirely dumb. He would never consider a case, in which you were representing a defendant, a dead open-and-shut case.''

"But," Mason said, "he sent this Donovan Fraser in to try the case unaided. Fraser is a young eager beaver, a relatively new trial deputy. He's anxious to win his spurs and prove himself, and he's probably a little more belligerent than he will be after he has had five more years of courtroom practice under his belt.

"Now, why did Hamilton Burger pick that particular trial deputy to oppose me? He has some veterans in the office who are remarkably good lawyers.''

"Isn't Fraser a good lawyer?''

"I think he is. The point is, he's relatively inexperienced, and in this business there are some things you can learn only as the result of experience.''

"That's the only reason you think he may be laying a trap for you?" Della Street asked.

"No, that's only one of the reasons," Mason said. "The thing that bothers me is that in preparing this case they have apparently taken so much for granted—and I don't think they'd do that."

"In what way?"

"For instance," Mason said, "this gun that they took from Ellen Robb is, as far as the case is concerned up to this point, simply a gun. Apparently they didn't make any effort to trace the registration of the gun. Now, I just can't understand that."

"Well, after all, they found it in her possession and they found that the test bullet matched the bullet found in Nadine Ellis' body.

"If you were district attorney, you'd call in any trial deputy who happened to be unattached and say, 'Here's a case you *can't* lose. Regardless of the fact that Perry Mason is on the other side, you can't possibly conceive of any set of facts that would keep a judge from binding the defendant over to the Superior Court on this sort of showing."

Mason nodded.

"Well?" Della Street asked.

"I'll grant all that," Mason said, "but somehow I have a feeling that they may be laying a trap. It's almost impossible to think that they wouldn't have taken the number of the gun and tried to trace it through its various owners. Now then, if . . . if they can trace that gun to my possession, then what happens?"

"Then," she said, "you're in the soup."

"That's what I'm thinking," Mason said.

"And if you're going to get in the soup," she said, "isn't it better to become righteously indignant in court and claim that someone has doctored the evidence, that someone has substituted the bullets, that the murder simply couldn't have been committed with the weapon that was found in the pos-session of Ellen Robb because you, yourself, had been the one who had handed her that weapon and you had handed it to her at a time that was *after* Ellen had gone to the yacht?"

"How do we know it was after?" Mason asked.

"Why, she—I see," Della Street said.

"In other words," Mason said, "suppose Ellen is smart. Suppose she came to my office and told me a story about having gone to the yacht looking for Nadine Ellis, that she couldn't find her, that she had a fight with George Anclitas and left The Big Barn, that she found a gun in her suitcase and doesn't know what to do with it. She would tell me all this *before* Nadine Ellis had been murdered. Then, after she had given me a good story and aroused my sympathy, she'd go out and murder Nadine and—"

"Could she have done that?" Della Street asked. "Did she have the time? Remember, we had her virtually under surveillance because you had Paul Drake put operatives on the job to act as bodyguards. You felt that someone might try to cause trouble."

"That's what I'm trying to remember," Mason said. "There was an interval from the time she left our office before the bodyguards picked her up. Now then, she could have gone out to the yacht and killed Nadine Ellis during that interval. Is she a smart little babe who's taking me for a ride, or is she the victim of some sort of a diabolical frame-up? And if it's a frame-up, how the devil *could* they have worked it? How much does Hamilton Burger, the district attorney, know? How much rope is he giving me, hoping I'll hang myself, and what are my duties in this situation in view of the fact that I'm supposed to represent my client and not disclose evidence against her?"

"That," Della Street said, "is a formidable list of questions."

"And a great deal depends on getting the right answers," Mason said.

"So what do we do?" Della Street asked.

"We get in my automobile and drive around somewhere, where no one will recognize us, ask us any questions or serve us with any subpoena or other documents until just before three-thirty. Then we go to court, and no matter what happens, we stall things along so that we don't have to reach any decisions until after court adjourns for the evening. Then we have until tomorrow morning to plan a course of conduct.''

Della Street nodded, pushed back her chair.

"And," Mason said, "when we get back to court at three-thirty this afternoon, *if* we should happen to find that Mr. Hamilton Burger, the district attorney himself, has entered the case, we'll know that it was an elaborate trap and that I've walked into it.''

Chapter 12

Perry Mason carefully timed his entrance to the courtroom so that it was only a few seconds before three-thirty when he opened the swinging doors.

The bailiff, who had been watching the clock and frowning, pressed a button signaling Judge Keyser that everything was in readiness.

Two newspaper reporters hurried toward Mason. "Mr. Mason, Mr. Mason—"

The bailiff pounded a gavel. "Everybody rise," he said.

Mason walked past the reporters and stood facing the flag as Judge Keyser took his place on the bench.

Judge Keyser said, "The Court would like to get this matter finished this afternoon if it is at all possible. Now, Mr. Redfield is here and ready to take the stand?"

"Yes, Your Honor," Fraser said, looking toward the door of the witness room.

The door opened. Alexander Redfield came in, accompanied by Hamilton Burger, the district attorney.

Mason noted the significance of Burger's presence but kept his face completely without expression.

Judge Keyser, however, showed some surprise. "You're appearing in this case, Mr. District Attorney?" he asked.

"Yes, Your Honor, in person," Hamilton Burger said.

The judge started to say something, then changed his mind, turned to Redfield, said, "Mr. Redfield, you have now had an opportunity to study that other bullet and compare it with test bullets fired from the weapon which has been introduced as People's Exhibit B. In your opinion as an expert, was that bullet fired from that weapon?"

"It was not," Alexander Redfield said.

Judge Keyser could not refrain from an involuntary ejaculation of surprise. "What!" he asked.

Redfield shook his head. "It was not fired from that weapon. It was fired from a Smith and Wesson .38-caliber revolver, but it was not fired from the weapon introduced as Exhibit B."

"But the other bullet was? The so-called second bullet?"

"That's right. The bullet in evidence as Exhibit C-1 was not fired from that weapon. The bullet in evidence as C-2 was fired from that weapon. Bearing in mind that we have simply designated those bullets as number one and two, the words first and second were only a designation used by the doctor in his testimony. It didn't indicate that the bullets were fired in that numerical sequence. Unfortunately, the bullet referred to by Dr. Calvert as the first bullet was entered in evidence as C-2 while the bullet he referred to as the second bullet became C-1 in evidence. In order to avoid further confusion, I wish to refer to each bullet specifically by its exhibit number."

Judge Keyser ran his hand along the top of his head, then looked down at Burger and over at Mason. "Does counsel on either side care to make any statement?"

Mason shook his head.

Hamilton Burger said, "We have no statement at this time, Your Honor."

"Now, just a moment," Judge Keyser said. "Let's be practical about this, Mr. District Attorney. The evidence so far shows unmistakably that a crime has been committed. There is evidence—or rather I should say there has been evidence—tending to show this defendant committed the crime. What might have been referred to as the fatal weapon was found in her possession. However, there are now certain unusual circumstances in this case.

"Because of a lapse of time and the start of putrefaction, it is impossible for the autopsy surgeon to tell which of two bullets was fired first. Either bullet could have caused death.

It is impossible for the autopsy surgeon to give an estimate as to the interval of time between the firing of the first and second shot. It has been at least intimated by the defense that a part of the defense in this case will be predicated upon the assumption that one of the bullets was fired a sufficient length of time after the other bullet so that death at least could have taken place prior to the time this bullet was fired.''

"I understand, Your Honor," Hamilton Burger said.

"I am assuming," Judge Keyser said, "that the position of the prosecution is that the point is immaterial as far as a preliminary hearing is concerned, that there is sufficient evidence tending to connect the defendant with the commission of the crime to result in her being bound over.

"I am forced to say that I consider this position to be well taken in the eyes of the law. However, from a practical standpoint the Court would have wished that the situation could have been cleared up. It is not a pleasant duty to bind a young woman over for trial, knowing that the interim must be spent in jail. Therefore, the Court would, for its own information, have liked to have had more light on the subject. However, if it is the position of the prosecution that technically the case calls for binding the defendant over, the Court feels that that position is probably well taken."

Mason arose and said somewhat deferentially, "I take it the Court is not precluding the defense from putting on evidence."

"Certainly not," Judge Keyser said, "but let's be realistic. With the circumstantial evidence which we have in this case, a weapon which at least could be the murder weapon, found in the possession of the defendant, you can hardly contend that the evidence doesn't at least connect the defendant sufficiently with the crime to result in an order binding her over regardless of what counter-showing you might make."

"I'm not prepared to make that concession, Your Honor," Mason said.

Hamilton Burger arose with a ponderous dignity. "May I be heard?" he asked.

"Certainly, Mr. District Attorney," Judge Keyser said, "although it seems to me that Mr. Mason has the laboring oar here."

"We are not finished with our case," the district attorney said, "and we have no intention of relying upon the evidence and the assumption as indicated by the Court. We expect to go further with our proof."

"You do?" Judge Keyser asked.

Hamilton Burger nodded.

Judge Keyser settled back on the bench. "Very well," he said. "I will state that the Court will welcome such proof. I had been hoping such proof would be adduced. That was the reason I continued the matter so we could get an opinion from Mr. Redfield. Proceed with your proof."

"I believe Mr. Mason was cross-examining the witness," Hamilton Burger said.

"That is right," Judge Keyser said. "Do you have any further questions on cross-examination, Mr. Mason?"

"I have several questions," Mason said.

"In that case," Hamilton Burger said, "I will ask permission of the Court to withdraw Mr. Redfield temporarily so that I may put on another witness who will, I believe, connect up the revolver, Exhibit B, in such a way that certain matters will be clarified. This is testimony which I am particularly anxious to introduce this afternoon."

"I have no objection," Mason said. "I would, in fact, prefer to defer my cross-examination of Mr. Redfield until this additional evidence is before the Court."

"Very well," Judge Keyser said. "So ordered. Go ahead, bring on your other witnesses, Mr. District Attorney."

Hamilton Burger said, "I call Darwin C. Gowrie to the stand."

An officer opened the door of the witness room, and Gowrie stepped into the room.

"Come forward and be sworn, Mr. Gowrie," Hamilton Burger said.

Gowrie held up his hand and was sworn.

"You are now and for some years past have been an attorney at law, practicing in the court of this state?"

"That is correct."

"I will ask you if you are acquainted with Perry Mason, the attorney for the defense?"

"I am."

"I will ask you if, on the ninth of this month, you had a conversation with Perry Mason over the telephone?"

"I did."

"At that time did Mr. Mason make some statements to you concerning certain unusual decisions in murder cases?"

"He did."

"What was the conversation?"

"Now, just a minute," Judge Keyser said. "I notice there is no objection on the part of the defense, but the Court hardly sees the relevancy of this."

"If the Court please," Hamilton Burger said, "I propose to connect this up. It is an important point in the prosecution's case which I wish to make."

"As part of a *preliminary* examination?" Judge Keyser asked.

"Exactly, Your Honor," Hamilton Burger said. "Without wishing to engage in personalities, I wish to state as an officer of this court that in the past I have felt there have been cases where defense counsel has gone far beyond the bounds of propriety in representing clients accused of crime. I may state to the Court that in several of those cases an investigation would have been made and disciplinary action quite possibly taken, only, as it happened, because of somewhat spectacular and highly dramatic developments, it turned out that the wrong person was being prosecuted for the crime. Under those circumstances it was felt that an investigation would hardly be worth while.

"However, in the present case evidence is at hand which

135

shows at least by inference *exactly* what happened, and we consider this evidence equally as important as evidence tending to connect the defendant with the commission of the crime. I may state that before we are finished with this evidence, we are going to show unmistakably a link which implicates counsel for the defense in this case, not as an attorney engaging in unethical methods, but as an actual accomplice—an accessory after the fact."

"Now, just a minute," Judge Keyser said. "That statement, Mr. District Attorney, will of course be widely publicized. The Court feels that it is unnecessary for you to make such a statement at this time."

"I merely wanted the Court to understand my position."

"Very well," Judge Keyser said, "the statement has been made now and it cannot be recalled. If the Court had had any idea of what you had in mind, the Court would have intervened and prevented the making of such statements. The Court was only asking you whether this proof was pertinent."

"It is pertinent. I wanted to show the Court how it was to be connected up."

"Very well, go ahead," Judge Keyser said. "I may state, however, Mr. District Attorney, that in the event the proof falls short of your statement, the Court will consider the making of such statement at this time as serious misconduct, perhaps amounting to a contempt of court."

"I am quite aware of the entire possibilities of the situation," Hamilton Burger said, "and I made my statement knowingly and after having given it careful thought. If I don't prove my point, I will willingly answer to charges of contempt."

"Very well, go ahead."

Hamilton Burger turned to the witness.

"Did you make notes of the conversation you had with Perry Mason?"

"Yes, sir."

"Why, may I ask?"

"Because the conversation was exceedingly unusual and very interesting as far as an attorney is concerned."

"What was the nature of that conversation?"

"Mr. Mason told me about certain legal points which were startlingly unusual and which he had investigated from time to time."

"What was the nature of the conversation in regard to those legal points?"

"Well, it came up because Mr. Mason had suggested to a client of mine that community property which had been lost in a gambling game could be recovered by the other spouse and restored to the community. It was a remarkably unusual doctrine, and I wanted to check with Mr. Mason to make certain I had not misunderstood him."

"Was there any other conversation?"

"Yes."

"Go ahead and relate the conversation."

"Well, Mr. Mason told me he hadn't been misunderstood, he confirmed a citation which certainly lays down a rather remarkable rule of law in regard to gambling."

"And then?" Hamilton Burger asked.

"Then he went on to tell me that he had a file which he kept of unusual decisions."

"Did he make a point in regard to murder?"

"Yes. He said that there were decisions to the effect that if a person fired a fatal bullet into a victim, that is, a bullet which would necessarily cause death, and then, before the victim actually expired, another individual fired a second bullet which resulted in death, the person firing the first bullet was not guilty of murder."

"Did he cite decisions?"

"He did. I made a note of those decisions because I was greatly interested."

"Now then, can you give us the time of the conversation as well as the date?"

"Yes, it happens that I can because my office keeps a note of the numbers that I call and the time consumed in

137

conversation. I found that I was spending a great deal of my time in telephone consultations for which we were making no charge and—''

"Never mind that," Hamilton Burger said. "I am asking if you can give the exact date and the exact time, and your answer was in the affirmative. Now, will you tell us the date and the time?"

"The call was made at nine-thirty on the morning of the ninth."

"Will you please give us the references Mr. Mason gave you at that time?"

"He referred to Dempsey versus State, 83 Ark. 81, 102 S.W. 704; People versus Ah Fat, 48 Cal. 61; Duque versus State, 56 Tex. Cr. 214; 119 S.W. 687."

"Cross-examine," Hamilton Burger said to Mason.

"How did you know you were talking with me on the telephone?" Mason asked.

"I called your office number, I asked the person answering the phone to have Mr. Mason put on the line, and you came on the line."

"You recognized my voice?"

"At the time, no. I had not heard your voice. Since then I have heard your voice and know that you were the party to whom I was talking over the telephone."

"You don't know where I was when I answered that telephone—this is, you don't know whether I was in my private office, in the reception room, in the law library or where I was."

"No, sir."

"And you don't know whether I was alone or whether anyone was with me."

"No, sir, *I* don't know."

"That's all," Mason said. "I have no further questions."

"Call your next witness," Judge Keyser said grimly.

"Call Lieutenant Tragg," Hamilton Burger said.

Lt. Tragg emerged from the witness room and took the stand.

"You took the defendant into custody on Thursday, the eleventh, Lieutenant?"

"I did."

"You had a warrant?"

"Yes."

"A search warrant?"

"Yes."

"Did you find a revolver in her possession?"

"Yes."

"Describe it, please."

"It was a Smith and Wesson .38-caliber police model with a two-and-a-half-inch barrel, blued steel, number 133347."

"I call your attention to People's Exhibit B and ask you if you have seen that gun before."

"I have. It is the gun I found in the possession of the defendant."

"Did you find any paper in her possession?"

"I did. I found this memo taken in shorthand. I can read the shorthand notes. They say '*Murder* cannot be proven if two guns used in crime inflicting equally fatal wounds at different times, Dempsey versus State, 83 Ar. 81, 102 S.W. 704; People versus Ah Fat, 48 Cal. 61; Duque versus State, 56 Tex. Cr. 214, 119 S.W. 687.'"

Hamilton Burger said, "I ask that this note be marked for identification as People's Exhibit G. I wish to keep the intervening letters free for other firearm exhibits so they may be in order. Presently I shall show this note is in the defendant's handwriting."

"No objections," Mason said.

"Cross-examine," Burger snapped.

"No questions," Mason said.

"Call Loring Crowder," Hamilton Burger said.

Once more the door of the witness room opened, and a well-groomed, rather chunky man in his late forties entered the courtroom, held up his hand, was sworn, took his seat in the witness chair, turned to Hamilton Burger.

"Your name is Loring Crowder," Hamilton Burger said.

"You are engaged in the retail liquor business, Mr. Crowder?"

"That is right."

"I'm going to show you a gun, Exhibit B in this case, numbered 133347, and ask you if you have ever seen that gun before."

Crowder took the gun, turned it over, looked at the numbers, said, "May I consult a memoranda?"

"You may," Hamilton Burger said, "if you will first tell us what it is."

"It is a notebook containing the number of a gun which I purchased from the Valleyview Hardware and Sporting Goods Store."

"Go ahead, consult the notebook," Hamilton Burger said.

Crowder looked at the notebook, then at the gun, said, "This is the same gun. I bought this gun about two and a half years ago from the store mentioned. I bought it to keep in my place of business."

"And what did you do with it?"

"I gave it to a friend about a year ago."

"Who was the friend?"

Crowder said, "I gave this gun to my friend, George Spencer Ranger. Mr. Ranger was having troubles and—"

"Never mind that," Hamilton Burger interrupted. "I'm just trying to trace the gun. You gave it to George Spencer Ranger."

"That is right."

"Was it a gift or a loan?"

"It was a loan."

"And did Mr. Ranger return the gun to you?"

"No, sir, he didn't. He told me that he had given it to—"

"Never mind what he told you. That's hearsay," Hamilton Burger said. "I'm simply asking you if he gave the gun back to you."

"No, sir, he did not."

"That's all," Hamilton Burger said. "Cross-examine."

"No questions," Mason said.

"Call George Spencer Ranger," Hamilton Burger said.

Once again an officer opened the door of the witness room, and Ranger, a tall, loose-jointed man in his forties with a shock of dark hair and heavy dark eyebrows, entered the courtroom.

"Hold up your right hand and be sworn," Hamilton Burger said.

The witness was duly sworn, gave his name and address to the court reporter, seated himself on the witness chair, turned to Judge Keyser and said, "I want it understood that I am here against my will. I have been subpoenaed by an officer who took me into custody and forced me to accompany him here. I am not testifying willingly."

"That doesn't make any difference at this time," Judge Keyser said. "If you were brought here in response to the process of the court, you are here and you are called as a witness. It is your duty to give your testimony."

"If the Court please," Hamilton Burger said, "this is a hostile witness. It will be necessary to ask leading questions."

"Go ahead with your examination," Judge Keyser said. "We will determine the attitude and the necessity for leading questions as we go along and if and when objection is made."

"You are acquainted with Loring Crowder?"

"I am, yes, sir."

"Did Loring Crowder lend you a Smith and Wesson revolver some time ago?"

The witness thought for a moment, then said, "Yes."

"Did you return that gun to Mr. Crowder?"

"I did not."

"Where is it now?"

"I don't know."

"What did you do with it?"

"I . . . I surrendered it."

"To whom?"

"My attorney told me it would be better to leave it with him."

"Who was your attorney?"

The witness hesitated.

"Who was it?" Hamilton Burger asked. "The court records show it. It was Perry Mason, wasn't it?"

"Yes."

"Now then, I show you a gun marked People's Exhibit B, being a Smith and Wesson revolver, number 133347, and ask you if that is the gun."

"I don't know," the witness said, giving the gun only a cursory look.

"Look at it," Hamilton Burger said. "Take it in your hand."

The witness extended his hand, looked at the gun, handed it back to Hamilton Burger, said, "I still don't know."

"All right, I'll put it this way," Hamilton Burger said. "You got a gun from Loring Crowder?"

"Yes."

"And whatever that gun was, you gave that gun to Perry Mason?"

"Yes."

"When?"

"When my case was coming up, something over six months ago."

"Did Perry Mason at any time ever give that gun back to you?"

"No."

"That was the last time you saw it, when you gave it to Perry Mason?"

"Yes."

"And the gun that you gave him was the same gun that you got from Loring Crowder?"

"Yes."

"Is there anything about this gun which is at all dissimilar to the gun which was given you by Loring Crowder?"

"I can't remember. I can't remember what that gun looked like."

"It could be this gun?"

"It could be."

"You may cross-examine," Hamilton Burger said.

"No questions," Mason said.

"Now," Hamilton Burger said, "I want to call Helman Ellis, the husband of the deceased woman."

Once more the door of the witness room was opened, and the deputy called out the name, "Helman Ellis."

Ellis entered the courtroom, glanced at Ellen Robb, hastily averted his eyes, walked over to take the oath and seated himself in the witness chair.

Hamilton Burger said, "You name is Helman Ellis. You were the husband of Nadine Ellis? She was your wife in her lifetime?"

"Yes."

"You own the yacht on which the body was found, the *Cap's Eyes*?"

"Yes."

"When did you last see your wife alive?"

"I saw her briefly on the early morning of Wednesday, the tenth."

"Where was she?"

"She was in our house, and then I last saw her in an automobile."

"Where?"

"At our home at Rowena, in the garage."

"Did you have any conversation with her?"

"A very brief conversation."

"And of what did that conversation consist?"

"I told her I wanted to explain certain things to her. She told me that an explanation could do no good, that things had progressed to such a point that talk would accomplish nothing."

"Then what?"

"I kept trying to patch things up with her, but I saw it was no use. I was trying to get possession of a gun she had. She told me she was going to divorce me."

"What time was that?"

"A little before six."

"Will you explain the circumstances, please?"

"The night before, that was Tuesday night, I had planned to go cruising on our yacht. She was going to accompany me. We had an argument. She pulled a gun on me and left me marooned on the yacht. She told me she was going to Arizona and kill 'my mistress.' I didn't get ashore until nine-thirty.

"After I warned Ellen, I went home and quietly let myself in. I slept on the couch without undressing. My wife latch-keyed the door and let herself in about 5:45 A.M. She had been driving our car. She left the motor running while she went to her room to get something.

"I followed her out to the car. She said she was satisfied I had tried to make her think 'my mistress,' the defendant, had gone to Arizona simply to throw her off the trail. She said she knew now where the defendant was and that I had spent the night with the defendant. She said the defendant had gone aboard our yacht in the belief I was there. She said she was going to pistol-whip the defendant so her beauty would be permanently marred."

"What did you say to that?"

"Nothing. I had never met the defendant aboard our yacht. I knew my wife was barking up the wrong tree, so I decided to let her go, feeling she might calm down after she found out her mistake.

"She had also told me she was going to have a fingerprint expert dust the cabin of the yacht to find the defendant's fingerprints. Since I felt sure there were no fingerprints of the defendant there, I felt it would be best to let my wife follow up this lead, and in that way she might convince herself her suspicions were groundless."

144

"Then what happened?"

"She drove off."

"And at that time she was headed for your yacht?"

"Yes."

"You never saw her alive after that?"

"No."

"Cross-examine," Burger said.

"Later on, on Wednesday, you went to my office?" Mason asked.

"Yes."

"And told me about the altercation on the yacht?"

"Yes."

"And about this subsequent meeting with your wife?"

"Yes."

"That's all," Mason said. "I have no further questions."

"Just a minute," Hamilton Burger said. "I have some questions on redirect."

Hamilton Burger arose and faced the witness. "Did you have occasion to look for your yacht, the *Cap's Eyes*, later on, on Wednesday?"

"Yes."

"At what time?"

"Around noon."

"Was it at its accustomed mooring at the club?"

"No, sir, it was gone."

"When did you next see it again?"

"When the police brought it back."

"When did you next see your wife again?"

"In the morgue."

"Now, I show you a gun which was found near the hand of your wife when her body was discovered on the yacht. I note that this gun is identical in appearance with the gun which has been introduced in evidence as People's Exhibit B, number 133347. Now, I don't like to keep referring to these weapons in the record by number, so I am simply going to refer to this as the Ellis gun because it was found in the cabin of your yacht and I believe you can identify that as to ownership.''

Ellis said, "I can, yes, sir. That gun was given to me by George Anclitas.''

"And what did you do with it? Did you carry it?''

"No, sir, I did not. I kept it aboard the yacht for personal protection.''

"Your wife knew it was there?''

"Yes.''

"Where was it customarily kept?''

"In a drawer in the cabin.''

"Do you know if you wife had this gun on Tuesday? Was that the gun you referred to when you testified your wife pulled a gun?''

"Yes, sir.''

Hamilton Burger said, "We ask that this gun be marked for identification as People's Exhibit E, Your Honor. We will not offer to introduce it in evidence at this time, because that offer should properly come after positive identification is made as to this being the gun that was found in the cabin of the yacht, the *Cap's Eyes*.''

"Very well,'' Judge Keyser said, "the gun will be marked for identification only.''

"I don't think I have any further questions at this time,'' Hamilton Burger said, "but I notice it is nearing the hour of adjournment. My next witness, George Anclitas, is here under subpoena. He is a businessman, proprietor of an establishment in Rowena, which has several businesses combined under one management, a motel, a trout pool, a swimming pool, a night club and a parlor where legalized games are played. It is a great hardship for Mr. Anclitas to be here, and I ask permission of the Court to withdraw this witness and put Mr. Anclitas on the stand at this time.

"The testimony of Mr. Anclitas will be brief, and in this way we can finish with him this afternoon so he won't have to return tomorrow.''

Judge Keyser looked inquiringly at Perry Mason. "Does the defense wish to object?" he asked.

"No objection," Mason said. "It is quite all right as far as I am concerned."

"Call George Anclitas."

The deputy opened the door of the witness room. George Anclitas emerged.

Helman Ellis, leaving the witness stand, walked in front of Ellen Robb, smiled reassuringly and returned to the witness room.

George Anclitas, his head held high, stalked to the witness stand with the stiff-backed gait of a marching soldier, turned with almost military precision, held up his hand, took the oath and seated himself.

"Your name is George Anclitas? You are one of the owners of The Big Barn in Rowena?" Hamilton Burger asked.

"Yes, sir."

"Do you know the defendant?"

"Yes, sir."

"Was she in your employ?"

"Yes, sir."

"For how long?"

"Some four or five months."

"And what were her duties?"

"She sang songs, sold cigars and cigarettes when necessary and did various odd jobs."

"When did the employment terminate?"

"She left on the evening of the ninth."

"Why did she leave?"

"I fired her."

"Why?"

Judge Keyser said, "Of course, this is preliminary but unless it's connected up I don't see its relevancy, particularly in view of the fact that the answer might tend to be an appraisal of the character of the defendant through hostile eyes."

"I think it's pertinent. I think it will be connected up, Your Honor," Hamilton Burger said.

"No objection from the defense," Mason said. "Let him go right ahead."

"Answer the question," Hamilton Burger said.

"She was bringing too much notoriety to the place. She was having an affair with Helman Ellis, and Mrs. Ellis got on to it—"

"Now, just a minute, just a minute," Judge Keyser said. "This witness is obviously testifying to hearsay now."

"I think perhaps these are conclusions of the witness, based upon his own personal observations, however," Hamilton Burger said.

"I think it's hearsay," Judge Keyser said. "Let *me* ask the witness a couple of questions. How do you know the defendant was having an affair with Helman Ellis?"

"Because I caught them."

"You caught them?"

"Well, they were embracing."

"How do you know that Mrs. Ellis knew about it?"

"Because she made a scene with the defendant, Ellen Robb."

"Were you there?"

"I was there."

Judge Keyser glanced down at Perry Mason, a puzzled frown creasing his forehead. "Very well," he said, "go ahead."

"Now then, did you give Helman Ellis a gun?"

"I did."

"What kind of a gun?"

"A Smith and Wesson, .38-caliber, two-and-a-half-inch barrel."

"I will show you a gun marked for identification as People's Exhibit E and ask you if that is the gun."

Anclitas looked at the gun, said, "That's the one."

"How long ago did you give him this gun?"

"About six weeks ago."

"Cross-examine," Hamilton Burger said.

Mason said, "Before embarking upon this cross-examination, Your Honor, I would like to ask whether test bullets from this gun marked Exhibit E were compared with the fatal bullet number one taken from the body of the decedent."

Judge Keyser nodded his head. "That seems a logical question. Were they so compared, Mr. District Attorney?"

"Certainly not," Hamilton Burger snapped.

"Why not?" Judge Keyser asked.

"Why should they be? This gun, Exhibit E, was fired *at* the assailant. A bullet from this gun was found embedded in the woodwork of the cabin near the door. It has only been fired once."

"Nevertheless," Judge Keyser said, "in view of the fact that it is now apparent that there is one bullet which can't be accounted for—at least we can't account for the gun which fired it—it would seem that there should be a ballistics test made of this weapon. I should think that would have been done as a matter of routine."

"At the time," Hamilton Burger said, "we were under the impression both of the fatal bullets had been fired from the gun which was in the possession of the defendant, the gun Exhibit B."

"I can readily understand that," Judge Keyser said, "but it certainly seems to me there should be a comparison of the other bullet, the slightly damaged bullet, with test bullets fired from this gun."

"Yes, Your Honor."

"It is now becoming apparent that we can't close this case today. I would suggest that the ballistics expert make such an examination before court convenes tomorrow morning."

"Yes, Your Honor," Hamilton Burger said.

"Now go ahead with your cross-examination, Mr. Mason."

Mason said, "There was an altercation with the defendant prior to her discharge?"

"I don't know what you mean, an altercation," Anclitas said. "She attacked me."

"In what way?"

"Striking and clawing."

"And you hit her?"

"I defended myself."

"You hit her?"

"I tell you, I defended myself."

"You hit her?"

"What was I supposed to do, stand there and let my face get clawed? I tried to keep her off."

"You hit her?"

"All right, I hit her!" Anclitas shouted.

"Thank you," Mason said. "I believe you hit her in the eye."

"I don't know where I hit her. I popped her one."

"You saw her with a black eye?"

"I saw her with a black eye."

"And you have been sued for seventy-five hundred dollars actual and punitive damages because of this assault you made on the defendant?"

"I object, Your Honor," Hamilton Burger said. "That's not proper cross-examination. It's incompetent, irrelevant and immaterial."

Judge Keyser, plainly interested, leaned forward to study George Anclitas. "The objection is overruled," he said. "It goes to show the bias of the witness."

"Answer the question," Mason said.

"All right, so I'm getting sued. Any lawyer can file a suit. She hasn't collected anything and she isn't going to."

"You propose to see to it that she doesn't collect?"

"That's exactly right. You just slapped a nuisance value suit on me, hoping I'd compromise. I've got news for you, Mr. Mason. You ain't going to get a dime."

"And as a result you don't like me?" Mason asked.

"Since you asked me the question and since I'm under

oath," Anclitas said, "I don't like any part of you. I don't like the ground you walk on."

"Now then," Mason said, "you took one look at this gun and said that was the gun you had given Helman Ellis."

"That's right."

"You didn't look at the number?"

"I didn't need to. I know the gun."

"What do you know about it?"

"Look," Anclitas said, "my partner bought four guns, Mr. Mason. He bought them all at once. He bought them from the Rowena Hunting and Fishing Store. He brought them to the place of business and gave them to me."

"Do you know the numbers?"

"Why should I know the numbers?" Anclitas asked in disgust. "I should go around carrying gun numbers in my head!"

"The guns were all alike?" Mason asked.

"All alike. It was a special order."

"Your partner went in and picked them up?"

"I placed the order, and then after the manager of the store told me the guns were in, I sent Slim Marcus down to pick them up."

"The guns were all identical in appearance?"

"That's right."

"Then how can you tell that this was the gun you gave Helman Ellis? How do you distinguish it from any of the other guns if you didn't look at the number?"

"Because I know the gun."

"How do you know it?" Mason asked. "What is distinctive about it? What differentiates it from any of the other guns?"

"Well, for one thing, this particular gun has a little nick on the front sight."

"Anything else?"

"I don't think so."

"Where are the other three guns?"

"I have them."

"Where?"

"At my place of business, naturally. I don't carry three guns with me, one in each hip pocket and one in the side coat pocket," Anclitas said sarcastically.

"If the Court please," Mason said, "I see it is approaching the hour of the afternoon adjournment. I would like to have the witness instructed to return to court tomorrow morning and bring those guns with him."

Hamilton Burger, his face flushed with indignation, was on his feet.

"Here we go again, Your Honor, a typical Perry Mason trick. It's a well-known fact that when Mason gets in a case he starts digging up guns out of anywhere and everywhere. He gets them in the case and juggles them all around and gets everybody confused. Those three guns that George Anclitas has have nothing more to do with this case than the stock of guns in the gun display counter in the Rowena Hunting and Fishing Store."

"I'm inclined to agree with the district attorney," Judge Keyser said. "I fail to see where they have any bearing in this case."

Mason said, "The witness has identified the gun that he gave Helman Ellis by stating that it had a slight nick in the front sight. There were no other marks of identification."

"Well, that one mark of identification is all he needs under the circumstances," Hamilton Burger blazed.

Mason abruptly pushed the gun into the district attorney's hands. "All right," he said, "if that's the way you feel about it, point out the nick in the front sight so the Court can see it."

Hamilton Burger shouted, "Point it out yourself! I'm not taking orders from you!"

"Then perhaps we'll let the witness point it out," Mason said. "I only suggested you do it because you were so positive that this mark of identification was sufficient. I will hand

152

the gun to the witness and ask him to point out the identifying mark on the front sight.''

Mason turned to Anclitas. "Perhaps, Mr. Anclitas, you'll be good enough to leave the witness stand, step up here and point out the notch or nick on the front sight to the Court and to the district attorney.''

"He can point it out to the Court," Hamilton Burger said. "He doesn't need to point it out to the district attorney. The district attorney knows what gun this is. The district attorney does want to state to the Court, however, that the greatest care should be taken to see that these tags marking the guns as Exhibits are not switched. At the moment, defense counsel has two guns in this case, and if he's given the faintest opportunity—''

"That will do," Judge Keyser interrupted coldly. "There is no occasion for such statements. The witness will step forward and point out the nick on the front sight of the gun to the Court.''

Anclitas came forward, said, "It isn't so much of a nick, really, just a place where the metal was scraped. We had an argument about whether a manicurist's nail file was hard enough to cut steel, and I drew the edge of the file along here. I—''

Abruptly Anclitas stopped, looked at the gun, then turned the gun over, held it to the light and said, "Well, I guess it wore off. It wasn't a deep cut in the metal, just a place where we'd sort of cut through the bluing on the steel.''

Judge Keyser leaned forward. "But I don't see *any* place where the bluing has been cut through.''

"Neither do I," Anclitas admitted.

"Yet," Perry Mason said, "this was the only mark of identification on which you said you relied in swearing under oath that this was the gun you had given Helman Ellis.''

"Well, it was found in his boat, wasn't it?''

"The question is," Mason said, "how *you* can be sure.''

Anclitas turned the gun over and over in his hand. "Well," he said, "I'm certain, that's all. I just know this is the gun but . . . well, I don't seem to see the place where the nail file left a mark on the front sight."

Mason, feeling his way cautiously, said, "Now, let me see if I understand you, Mr. Anclitas. You bought four guns at one time?"

"That's right."

"And one of those guns you gave to Helman Ellis?"

"I've already said so half a dozen times."

"And there was a dispute as to whether an ordinary manicurist's nail file was hard enough to leave a mark on a gun barrel?"

"Yes, sir."

"And was a bet made on that?"

"Yes, sir."

"With whom?"

"With my partner, Slim Marcus."

"How much was the bet?"

"Fifty dollars."

"Do you remember how the subject came up?"

"Oh, Your Honor," Hamilton Burger said, "this is completely incompetent, irrelevant and immaterial. It's not proper cross-examination. Counsel is quite obviously simply trying to prolong proceedings past the hour of adjournment, hoping that during the evening he can think of some more questions to ask Mr. Anclitas.

"I have already pointed out that it would be inconvenient for Mr. Anclitas to return to—"

Judge Keyser interrupted. "We still have a few minutes, Mr. District Attorney. The question of the identification of this gun having been opened up, and the witness having stated that he identified it solely from the mark of a manicurist's nail file left in the front sight, I certainly think counsel is within his rights. The objection is overruled. Answer the question, Mr. Anclitas."

"Well," Anclitas said, "we were talking about the different guns and I suggested they should be marked, that we had four guns and there was no way of telling one from the other unless we looked at the numbers. So I suggested we file little marks on the barrel of the guns; one mark on one gun, two on the next, three on the next and four on the other.

"Slim Marcus, my partner, thought it was a good idea, but we couldn't find a file so I said we'd go over to the barbershop and borrow a nail file from the manicurist, and he said a nail file wasn't hard enough to cut the barrel of a gun. I got in an argument about it and bet him fifty dollars."

"So what happened?" Mason asked.

"So we took the gun, went over to the barbershop, borrowed the manicurist's file, made the mark on the front sight of the gun, and I collected fifty dollars."

"Thereafter was your idea carried out, of marking each of the guns?"

"No. Slim was mad over losing the bet and thought that I had framed the whole deal. He accused me of having experimented in advance of making the bet."

"Now, you state that this gun which had the mark on the front sight was the one that you gave Helman Ellis?"

"I certainly thought it was."

"What were the circumstances?"

"Well, after we had this bet I was carrying the gun back to the bar. It was a gun we kept underneath the bar just below the cash register so that in case of a holdup we could protect ourselves.

"Helman Ellis was standing there by the bar and saw me carrying the gun and wanted to know if I had been trying to make a collection from some customer who didn't want to pay or something of the sort—he made some joke about it, and one thing led to another and he started admiring the gun and finally I gave it to him. I felt it would be good business. Helman Ellis was becoming a regular customer and—well, I make no secret of it, I wanted to cultivate him.''

"Why?'' Mason asked.

"Because,'' Anclitas said angrily, "I'm running a place of business and I make a profit by having customers.''

"Then in your mind there was no question whatever but that the weapon you gave Helman Ellis was the one that had the file mark on the front sight?''

"That's right.''

"Yet you don't find this mark on the front sight here now, and therefore I take it you wish to change your statement that this was the gun you gave Helman Ellis?''

"I'm not changing anything,'' Anclitas said sullenly. "That's the gun that was found on the Ellis boat; it's the gun I gave Ellis.''

"But the distinguishing mark is no longer on the front sight.''

"It may have worn off.''

"You had no other means of identifying the gun?''

"Just by its appearance.''

"When you testified, you gave as your sole reason for identifying the gun—''

"Your Honor,'' Hamilton Burger interrupted, "this question has been asked and answered half a dozen times. The witness has given his best opinion. We now know the facts. We aren't going to gain anything by having counsel carry on an argument with this witness. I—''

A deputy who had hurried into the courtroom moved up to Hamilton Burger and tugged at his coat sleeve.

Burger turned in annoyance, saw the expression on the deputy's face, said to the judge, "Just a moment, please, Your Honor. May I be indulged for just a few minutes? Apparently a matter of some importance has arisen.''

Burger engaged in a whispered conference with the deputy. At first Burger's face showed complete incredulity, then surprise, then as the deputy continued to whisper forcefully, a slow grin began to appear on the district attorney's face.

Abruptly he nodded to the deputy, turned to the Court.

"If the Court please," he said, "a matter of transcendent importance has arisen in this case. I am going to call Perry Mason to the stand as my next witness."

"You can't do that," Judge Keyser said, then at the expression on Hamilton Burger's face, said, "unless, of course, there is some factual matter which can be cleared up by defense counsel. But certainly defense counsel is hardly qualified as a witness to appear against his client."

"As it happens, Your Honor," Hamilton Burger said, "and in order to explain the reason for my action, it seems that one Maurice Halstead, a very competent firearms expert engaged in ballistic examinations, was given a gun by Perry Mason's representative and was asked to fire several test bullets from that gun.

"When it appeared that there was some question about the two bullets in this case having been fired from different guns, Mr. Halstead communicated with my office to state that, while he wished to protect his relations with his client, he did not wish to be put in the position of concealing evidence. He asked that Mr. Redfield, the ballistics expert who has already testified in this case, make a confidential examination of the test bullets. If they had not been fired from the murder weapon, he asked that Mr. Redfield say nothing about the matter. If, on the other hand, they had been so fired and therefore were evidence, Maurice Halstead did not care to be put in the position of suppressing evidence."

Burger turned to Perry Mason and said significantly, "It is unfortunate that all persons are not actuated by such high standards of professional conduct."

Judge Keyser, plainly interested, was leaning forward. "Go on, Mr. District Attorney. Kindly avoid personalities. Make any statement that you wish to the Court, since this is a case being tried without a jury."

"The test bullets fired from the gun given Maurice Halstead by Perry Mason are an undoubted match with the bullet which we have referred to as bullet number two in this case, the one which previously we had been unable to identify.

"We now have a situation, Your Honor, where it appears that one fatal bullet was fired from a weapon which was in the possession of Perry Mason, that the second bullet—which *may* have been fired some time after death—was fired from a gun which had been in the custody of Mr. Perry Mason.

"The inference is obvious. The defendant in this case came to Perry Mason with a gun which had fired a fatal bullet into the body of Nadine Ellis. I won't at this time make any accusations, but it seems that that gun very mysteriously left the possession of the defendant and that the defendant was given a gun which could only have been given her by her counsel, Perry Mason. And it is at least an inference that she was instructed to return to the scene of the crime and fire a second bullet from that gun into the body of the victim.

"This, coming at a time when counsel had recently been investigating the law concerning two persons firing fatal shots into a body, certainly tells its own story.

"It is one thing for counsel to advise a person accused of crime and try to protect the rights of that person, but it is quite another thing for an attorney to become an accessory to murder.

"Counsel has been under suspicion before. This time by a fortunate circumstance the evidence exists which has—"

"That will do, Mr. District Attorney," Judge Keyser interrupted. "You will make no statements about counsel. If you have any matter to take before the Grievance Committee of the Bar Association, you may do so. If you wish to subpoena counsel to appear before the grand jury and have the grand jury investigate the question of whether counsel has become an accessory after the fact, you also have that privilege.

"In this court you are confined to discussing the relevancy of evidence. However, I will state that the statement you have made is certainly ample foundation to enable you to call Mr. Mason to the stand.

"Mr. Mason will take the stand and be sworn as a witness on behalf of the prosecution."

"Just a moment, Your Honor," Mason said, his face granite hard. "Regardless of what the district attorney may wish to prove by me, the fact remains that I am representing the defendant in this case and am entitled to conduct this case in an orderly manner. The witness, George Anclitas, is being cross-examined by me. The witness was called out of order on the statement of the district attorney that it would work a great hardship on him to be forced to return tomorrow. I insist on concluding my cross-examination of the witness."

"And I submit, if the Court please," Hamilton Burger said angrily, "that this is simply an excuse to stall for time. Counsel has actually completed his cross-examination. Any questions he may ask from now on will be purely repetitious."

"It would seem that the examination had reached a logical conclusion," Judge Keyser said. "The Court will state it does not intend to have this cross-examination unduly prolonged. However, counsel is certainly within his rights. The witness Anclitas was put on out of order on the representation of the district attorney that it would work a great hardship on him to have to return tomorrow. Counsel is entitled to complete his cross-examination before any other witness is called, particularly in view of the fact that this witness was put on out of order at the request of the district attorney."

Hamilton Burger yielded the point with poor grace. "I serve notice here and now," he said, "that I am going to insist this cross-examination be conducted within the strict rules of evidence and not used as an excuse to prolong this case."

"Very well," Judge Keyser said, "proceed with your questions, Mr. Mason."

"You are positive that the gun you gave Helman Ellis was the one that you had personally marked with a manicurist's nail file?" Mason asked.

"Objected to as already asked and answered and not proper cross-examination," Hamilton Burger said.

"Sustained," Judge Keyser snapped.

"When this gun was handed to you by the district attorney," Mason said, "when was the last time prior to that occasion that you had seen the weapon?"

"Objected to as already asked and answered and not proper cross-examination."

"Overruled."

"Answer the question," Mason said.

"When I gave the gun to Helman Ellis."

"You're satisfied it's the same gun?"

"Objected to as repetitious, as already asked and answered."

"Sustained."

"You don't know the various numbers on the four guns which you purchased?"

"Objected to as incompetent, irrelevant and immaterial; not proper cross-examination, already asked and answered," Burger said.

"The objection is sustained," Judge Keyser ruled.

"Do you now, or did you at the time you gave the weapon to Helman Ellis, know the number of that weapon?"

"Objected to as incompetent, irrelevant and immaterial; not proper cross-examination."

"The objection is overruled."

"No, I didn't know the number of that particular gun," Anclitas said. "I didn't look at it. I told you all I know. I gave him the gun. That's all I know."

160

"Have you had occasion to examine the other three guns remaining in your possession?" Mason asked.

"Objected to. Not proper cross-examination," Hamilton Burger said.

"Overruled."

"No, I haven't examined them."

"I would suggest," Mason said, "that during the evening adjournment you examine these guns carefully and see if any one of those three guns does have a mark on the front sight—a mark made by a nail file such as you have described."

"That's counsel's suggestion," Hamilton Burger said, "but you don't have to act on it. I submit to the Court that this witness has given his evidence to the best of his ability."

"There may, however, have been a confusion in the mind of the witness as to the sequence of events," Judge Keyser said. "I think it is established that he gave *a* gun to Helman Ellis. The gun found near the body of Nadine Ellis was a gun which had been sold to George Anclitas or his associate, Wilton Marcus. The Court is not very greatly impressed by any of these questions concerning the mark on the front sight. It is quite apparent that the witness made a perfectly natural mistake in regard to the sequence of events, and unless it can be shown that there is some significance which is not presently apparent, the Court is not impressed by the absence of a file mark on the front sight. If, however, it should appear that such a mark *is* on the front sight of one of the three guns remaining in the possession of this witness, it might clarify the situation simply by showing that there was a natural mistake.

"However, the Court fails to see where it affects the issues in this case other than, perhaps, to lay a foundation for cross-examining the witness when the matter reaches the Superior Court."

"Now then," Mason said, "I want to account for each one of these weapons. You purchased four weapons. I want to know where you kept them."

"Your Honor," Hamilton Burger said, "may I object, may I *please* object? This is not proper cross-examination. If counsel is permitted to go into the location of each of these four weapons and cross-examination the witness as to how he knows they're the same weapons, how he knows they were at a certain place at a certain time, this whole situation will become completely interminable. Counsel is very apparently stalling for time, and time is running out. It is now only a few minutes before the hour of the evening adjournment."

"Nevertheless," Judge Keyser said, "while the Court intends to be very strict in enforcing the rules of evidence and of cross-examination, the Court is not going to deprive the defendant of her rights simply because a situation has arisen in which defense counsel may well wish for time in order to prepare himself.

"The Court wishes to point out to the prosecutor that if the prosecutor had called Perry Mason to the stand without making this statement in open court, there would have been no opportunity for what the district attorney refers to as stalling."

"I thought I was within my rights in calling him," Hamilton Burger admitted somewhat sheepishly. "I had forgotten that technically he hadn't concluded his cross-examination of George Anclitas."

"That," Judge Keyser said coldly, "was your mistake, not the mistake of the Court. The Court wants to be fair in the matter. The Court will admit that in the face of statements made which apparently have been checked by the prosecutors, the circumstantial evidence indicates a situation of the utmost gravity. The Court will state further that the Court is going to get at the bottom of this and, while the Court intends to permit a reasonable cross-examination of this witness, the Court does not intend to have it unduly prolonged and the Court has now made up its mind that in the event it becomes necessary to take an evening adjournment, the Court is going to have a night session so that this matter can be disposed of without a delay which might tend to prejudice the rights of the parties.

"Now then, Mr. Mason, proceed with your cross-examination. The witness will answer the question. The objection is overruled."

"Will the court reporter read the question?" Mason asked.

The court reporter consulted his records, read the question to the witness: "Now then, I want to account for each one of these weapons. You purchased four weapons. I want to know where you kept them."

"We kept one gun by the cash register at the bar," Anclitas said. "We had one by the registration desk in the motel, and one was in the gaming room."

"You mean the gambling room?" Mason asked.

"I mean the gaming room."

"Where was the other?"

"The other was an extra. Sometimes I carried it when I was taking some money home with me. Sometimes I didn't. It was just sort of hanging around and—well, I guess you could call it an extra. That's why I gave it to Ellis."

"Did you endeavor to keep these guns separate in any way?" Mason asked. "Did you have any designation, either on the gun or on the holster?"

"There wasn't any holster—just the gun lying there where a person could grab it quick if he had to."

"And there was no attempt to designate them? That is, to differentiate one from the other?"

"Only this time that I told you about when we thought we could put some marks on them and then changed our minds."

"Within the last month," Mason said, "have you had any trouble over locating these guns? Has there been any element of confusion at any time within the last month?"

"None whatever," Anclitas said.

"Has one of the guns at any time been missing from its accustomed place?"

"Not that I know of."

"You state that you sometimes carried one of these weapons when you were carrying a large amount of money."

"That's right."

"Does any other person, or did any other person, carry one of those weapons under similar conditions?"

"My partner, Slim, carried one."

"Anyone else?"

"No one else. . . . Now, wait a minute. I think one of the hat-check girls who sometimes stayed at her mother's house and had to go home late at night, carried one for a couple of nights. I stopped her as soon as I found out what she was doing."

"You mean she carried one with her while she was on the job?"

"No, no. She had to take a bus and sometimes when she'd get off—around one or two o'clock in the morning— she was nervous about walking the six blocks to the place where she caught the bus and while she was waiting there. She tried to time her departure so she could leave and catch the bus right on the nose but she didn't dare miss the bus so she had to leave a little early to give herself a margin and sometimes the bus would be a little late. She had an embarrassing experience one night with an exhibitionist and . . . well, she just started borrowing one of the guns to take in her purse."

"Without telling you anything about it?"

"That's right."

"How did you find out about it?"

"She left her purse in the washroom. The attendant didn't know whose purse it was and took it to the office. I opened it to look for identification and found it was this girl's purse and a gun was in it. It looked like one of our guns, and I called her in the office and asked her about it, and then she admitted that she'd borrowed one from behind the counter."

"And you put a stop to it?"

"Sure I put a stop to it. She didn't have any permit to carry the gun in the first place, and in the second place suppose *we'd* been held up and the men behind the bar had reached down for the gun and there wouldn't have been any gun there?''

"But she brought the gun back whenever she took it?''

"Objected to as calling for a conclusion of the witness, as calling for hearsay evidence and not being proper cross-examination. It is incompetent, irrelevant and immaterial," Burger said.

"The objection is sustained," Judge Keyser ruled.

"What is the name of this young woman who borrowed the gun on occasion?''

"She's the hat-check girl.''

"What's her name?''

"Sadie Bradford.''

"Were there any witnesses present when you gave this gun to Helman Ellis?''

"Only my partner, Slim Marcus.''

"And you state that Slim Marcus on occasion carried one of the guns?''

"Objected to as already asked and answered," Hamilton Burger said.

"Sustained," Judge Keyser snapped.

"And aside from this one file mark on the front sight of the gun which you think you gave Ellis, there were no identifying marks on any of the guns. Is that right?''

"Objected to as already asked and answered. Incompetent, irrelevant and immaterial. Not proper cross-examination," Burger said.

"Sustained," Judge Keyser snapped.

Mason glanced at the clock. "I have no further questions of this witness," he said.

Hamilton Burger was instantly on his feet. "Call Perry Mason as a witness for the prosecution.''

"Take the stand, Mr. Mason," Judge Keyser said.

"Just a moment, Your Honor," Mason said. "I think counsel is forgetting, and perhaps the Court has overlooked the fact, that when Anclitas was put on the witness stand at the request of the district attorney, who wanted to eliminate the necessity of further attendance by Mr. Anclitas, the witness Helman Ellis was on the stand."

"I had concluded my examination of Mr. Ellis," Hamilton Burger said.

"I don't think the record so shows," Mason said. "I think instead the record shows that you said you thought you would have no more questions of that witness at that time."

"All right, I'll announce now, then, that I have concluded with that witness and I ask Mr. Mason to take the stand."

"Just a minute," Mason said. "I haven't had an opportunity to examine Mr. Ellis on re-cross-examination. If you have concluded your redirect examination I want to cross-examine him."

"You don't have anything to cross-examine him about," Hamilton Burger exploded. "All he testified to on redirect was that he had been given a gun by George Anclitas and he kept it on the yacht."

"I want to cross-examine him on that," Mason said.

"And I want you on the witness stand before you've had a chance to concoct any alibi," Hamilton Burger shouted.

"It is your contention that I am to be deprived of my right to cross-examine Mr. Ellis?"

Hamilton Burger took a deep breath. "Very well," he said, "I'll stipulate that the entire testimony of Helman Ellis may go out. I'll withdraw him as a witness. I'll strike all of his evidence out of the record."

"I won't agree to that," Mason said. "I won't so stipulate."

"Why not?"

"Because I want to cross-examine him."

Hamilton Burger glowered at Mason, then turned toward the Court.

Judge Keyser said, "It is past the hour of the evening adjournment by some minutes, Mr. Burger. I can appreciate the prosecutor's position, but the fact remains that the defense attorney has the right to cross-examine all witnesses called by the prosecution.

"Because I have some commitments and pre-trial conferences at this time and because I know some of the officers of the court have engagements, I am going to adjourn court at this time but I am going to reconvene at eight o'clock tonight. We are going to have an evening session. I think under the circumstances the prosecution is entitled to have its case presented expeditiously."

"The defense objects," Mason said. "It is inconvenient for me personally, and I feel that the defendant is being deprived of her rights."

Judge Keyser shook his head. "I'm not going to permit any technicalities to stand in the way of getting this matter disposed of. The Court will take a recess until eight o'clock this evening, at which time all persons under subpoena in this case will return to the courtroom.

"Court's adjourned."

Chapter 13

Mason paced the office floor in frowning concentration.

Della Street presided over an electric coffee percolator. A paper bag of doughnuts was on the office desk.

From time to time Mason would stop, take a few sips from a cup of coffee and munch on a doughnut.

"You're going to need something more nourishing than that," Della Street said anxiously. "Let me go down to the restaurant and get you a ham sandwich or a hamburger or—"

Mason motioned her to silence with a wave of his hand, once more resumed his pacing of the floor.

After nearly a minute he said absentmindedly, "Thanks, Della." And then after some two minutes added, "I've got to think."

"Can I help by asking questions?"

"Try it," Mason said. "No, wait a minute. *I'll* ask *you* the questions. You give me the answers. Let's see if I can detect anything wrong."

She nodded.

Mason whirled abruptly, stood facing her with his feet spread apart, his shoulders squared, his manner one that he sometimes used in cross-examining a witness.

"That gun Ellen Robb had," he said, "was locked in our safe from the time Ellen Robb entered the office until we returned it with one exception—when Drake took it to the ballistics expert. Now then, how could a bullet from that gun be in Nadine Ellis' body unless Ellen Robb fired it there?"

"It couldn't," Della Street said. "The time has come,

168

Chief, when you've got to throw your client overboard. She's committed murder and she's lied to you.''

"Now then,'' Mason went on without noticing Della Street's answer, "I took a gun out of my safe, a gun that we'll call the Loring Crowder gun. She put that gun in her purse. A bullet from *that* gun was *also* found in the body of Nadine Ellis. *How* did it get there?''

"The bullet was fired from the gun,'' Della Street said, "that's how it got there,'' and then added quickly, "not that I'm trying to be facetious, Chief. I'm just pointing out that the striation marks on the bullets show that it was fired from that gun. We have to face facts and we may as well face them now.''

"All right,'' Mason said, "it was fired from that gun. Who fired it?''

"Ellen Robb *had* to fire it.''

Mason said, "One thing we know for a fact and that is, the bullets couldn't have been fired simultaneously. They must have been fired after a very considerable time interval, probably an interval of hours. That's one thing *we* know that the police and the district attorney don't know. We have that much of an advantage.''

"Why is it an advantage?'' Della Street asked.

"Because we know something about sequence. We know that the bullet from the Crowder gun must have been fired into Nadine Ellis' dead body. Now then, once we establish that, Della, I'm not tied up with anything except being an accessory to having fired a bullet into a dead body. That's perhaps a misdemeanor—I haven't looked it up. Certainly it isn't homicide of any sort or an attempt to commit homicide.''

Della Street nodded.

"On the other hand,'' Mason said, "I'm hoist by my own petard. Here I have been talking about this freak decision that holds that it's not murder to fire a bullet that would prove fatal into the body of a victim, if some independent agency fires another bullet into the victim and that second bullet results in death. I am assuming, of course, that the first person could be charged with assault with intent to commit murder. However, because I dug out these decisions, no one is going to believe anything *I* may say. The sequence is too, too damning. It looks as if I had tried to save a client by legal skulduggery and the juggling of evidence.''

Della Street said, ''Ellen Robb was sitting right here in the office when you were talking on the telephone with Darwin C. Gowrie, the attorney for Nadine Ellis. She heard you tell all about the subtle distinction in the decisions. She made notes in shorthand. You weren't advising her, you were advising Gowrie.

''Let's assume Ellen is a very smart young woman. She had killed Nadine Ellis with one shot fired from the gun which she said she had found in her baggage. When you juggled guns on her she knew it, and she took advantage of your attempt to aid her by taking the second gun—the Crowder gun which you had substituted in place of the gun she had when she entered the office—and went out and fired a second bullet into the body of Nadine Ellis.''

Mason suddenly snapped his fingers. ''We're overlooking one thing,'' he said. ''We may have the time element *all* cockeyed.''

''How come?'' she asked.

''Suppose,'' Mason said, ''the bullet from the Anclitas gun was fired into Nadine Ellis' body *after* the bullet from the Crowder gun?''

''It couldn't have been,'' Della Street said.

''Why not?''

''Because that gun was locked in our safe after you gave the Crowder gun to Ellen Robb.''

''No, it wasn't,'' Mason said. ''There's one very suspicious circumstance about that gun which we're overlooking. We took it down to Anclitas' place and planted it in the women's room.''

Della Street's eyes became animated.

''Suppose we do have the order of the bullet wounds reversed,'' she exclaimed. "Suppose the first bullet was from the Crowder gun. Then the second bullet must have been from the Anclitas gun."

Mason nodded.

"Then you mean *after* the gun was returned to the powder room, George Anclitas took the gun, went out and fired a second shot into the dead body of Nadine Ellis?"

Mason nodded.

Della Street's eyes were sparking now. "That would account for the fact that he said nothing about having found the gun in the powder room. He must have missed it and must have had a pretty good idea of what had happened."

"What had happened?" Mason asked.

"That Ellen Robb had killed Nadine Ellis with it."

"But if this theory is correct," Mason said, "she wasn't killed with that gun. She was killed with the Crowder gun."

"All right," Della Street said, "we won't try to figure out how George knew Nadine Ellis was dead. But he did, for reasons of his own, take that gun, go out and fire another bullet into the dead body of Nadine Ellis."

"Now, wait a minute," Mason said. "You say he went out and did it. Remember that Nadine Ellis was out on a yacht and, figuring the dry fuel tank, the fact that the fuel tank had been filled when Helman Ellis and his wife were planning to take a cruise, the location of the boat, the yacht must have been out at sea for some time, and it would have been a physical impossibility for Anclitas to have taken the gun after we returned it, found the yacht and fired the second bullet. But if that had happened, the marks I made in the barrel with the etching tool would show up. Redfield would have noticed them."

"Then," Della Street said, suddenly discouraged, "it *must* have been done before, and your client has to be the one who did it."

Mason shook his head. "I'm still fighting for my client, Della."

Della Street said, "She's a millstone around your neck.

You'd better cut her loose and start swimming. After all, you acted in good faith. You thought that Anclitas had planted a gun in her things and was going to accuse her of stealing that gun. You wanted to cross him up.''

Mason nodded. ''I wanted to handle the situation in such a dramatic manner that we would teach George Anclitas a lesson,'' he said. ''You can see how my unorthodox tactics backfired.''

''But can't you explain what you were trying to do when you get on the witness stand?''

''Sure, I can explain,'' Mason said, ''but no one is going to believe me. Bear in mind that I had previously pointed out that when two independent agencies fired bullets into a body, only the person firing the last shot was guilty of murder, provided the first shot hadn't proven instantly fatal.

''The circumstantial evidence certainly indicates that Ellen Robb came to me, that she told me she had killed Nadine Ellis, that I told her to give me the gun, that I gave her another gun and told her to go out and fire another shot into the body of Nadine Ellis, that I intended to use my trick defense. Also that I then went back and planted the gun in George Anclitas' place of business hoping that he would make a commotion about it and I could involve him in the murder.''

''Well, what *are* you going to do?'' Della Street asked.

''I wish I knew,'' Mason said. ''All I know is, I'm going to go down fighting and I'm not going to throw my client overboard.''

''Not even to save your own skin?''

Mason shook his head.

''You'll be disbarred.''

''All right then,'' Mason said. ''I'll find some other line of work. I'm not going to betray a client. That's final.''

''Not even to tell the true facts?''

''I'll have to tell the true *facts*,'' Mason said. ''I can keep them from finding out what my client told me. Any conversations we had are privileged communications. As my secretary you share in the professional privilege. They can't make me tell anything that my client said for the purpose of getting me to take the case or any advice that I gave her.''

"But they can ask you if you substituted guns?'' Della Street asked.

"There,'' Mason said, "I'm stuck. Unless I refuse to answer on the ground that to do so would incriminate me.''

"Well, why not do that? They can't prove anything except by inference.''

Paul Drake's code knock sounded on the exit door of Mason's private office, and Mason nodded to Della Street. "Let Paul in, Della. Let's see what he knows, if anything.''

Della Street opened the door.

Paul Drake, looking as lugubrious as a poker player who has failed to fill a straight which was open at both ends, sized up the situation, said, "Hi, folks,'' walked over to the paper bag, abstracted a doughnut and accepted the cup of coffee that Della Street handed him.

"Well?'' Mason asked.

Drake shook his head. "This is the end of the road, Perry.''

"What do you know?'' Mason asked.

"This time you have a client who really and truly lied to you. She's in it up to her beautiful eyebrows and she's dragged you in it with her.''

"How come?'' Mason asked.

Drake said, "She and Helman Ellis were really ga-ga. Anclitas is telling the truth.''

"Go on,'' Mason said, as Drake paused as though groping for the right words in which to go on.

"You remember,'' Drake said, "when Ellen Robb came to you after she had been thrown out of The Big Barn and had the shiner?''

Mason nodded.

"She told you she had taken a taxi to the Surf and Sea Motel and you told her to go back there?''

Again Mason nodded.

"Well,'' Drake said, "when she first went to the Surf and Sea Motel, it was to meet Helman Ellis.''

Mason resumed pacing the floor. "How long was Ellis there?" he asked Drake.

"About half an hour."

Suddenly Mason shook his head. "That doesn't mean necessarily that my client was lying," he said. "It means that Helman Ellis was following her."

Drake said, "This is the part that hurts, Perry. He wasn't following her. He arrived before she did."

"What?"

"That's right."

"How do you know?"

"My operative talked with the man who runs the place. Now that Ellen Robb has been arrested, he's beginning to think back in his own mind, trying to recall things that would indicate either that Ellen was an innocent young woman who is being framed or that she was guilty. He's naturally interested in the whole situation and he remembered that before Ellen Robb showed up on Tuesday night, a car drove up to the motel, turned in at the entrance, circled through the grounds and then went out, as though the driver might have been looking for someone. At first he thought the man was going to register and ask for a room, so when the car slowed down, this manager jotted down the license number on a scratch pad."

"The license number?" Mason asked.

"That's right," Drake said. "You know the way they register in motels. The man writes down his name and address and the make and model of his car and the license number.

"Nine people out of ten forget the license number and it's something of a nuisance because the manager has to go out and look at the license plate and jot down the number. So this fellow keeps a pad of scratch paper by the desk, and when a car drives in, there's a powerful light shining on the car from the porch of the office. The manager automatically jots down the license number and then when the people register he doesn't have to go out and look at the license number in case they've forgotten it. And in case they give him a phony license number, he knows it immediately and can be on his guard."

"Go on," Mason said.

"Well, the manager jotted down the guy's license number. Then the fellow didn't come in to ask for a room but turned around, drove out front and parked. So the manager tore off the sheet of paper containing the license number, crumpled it and started to put it in the wastebasket. Then he thought perhaps the man was waiting for a woman companion to show up so he smoothed the piece of paper out again and put it in his desk drawer.

"Well, about ten minutes later Ellen Robb showed up in a taxi. The manager took her registration and assigned her to a cabin."

"And then he saw Ellis come and join her?" Mason asked.

"No, he didn't," Drake said, "but he did see Ellis get out of the car and walk up to the motel, apparently going in to call on somebody, and the manager *assumed* it was Ellen Robb, the unescorted woman who had registered."

"And so the manager did what?" Mason asked.

"Did nothing," Drake said. "After all, motels aren't conducted along the lines of young women's seminaries, and the manager isn't in any position to censor a young woman's callers. If he tried to do that, he'd be involved in more damage suits than you could shake a stick at, and the motel would be out of business in about two weeks. Motel managers have to take things as they come. All they watch out for is that people don't get noisy and make a nuisance out of themselves or that some woman doesn't move in and start soliciting. Even in that event they're pretty cautious, but there are certain things that give them a tip-off in cases of that sort. That type of woman usually has a certain appearance that the manager can detect, and they almost invariably work in pairs."

"All right, give me the rest of it," Mason said. "How bad it is?"

"Plenty bad," Drake said, "and the worst of it is, my man is the one who uncovered it."

"What do you mean?"

"Well, he was trying to dig up something that would help so he went down to the manager of the motel and started talking with him and asking him questions about Ellen Robb. You see, we got a bodyguard for her, Perry, but there was almost a full day before the bodyguard got there and—well, if anything phony had been pulled, that was when it must have been pulled, so my man started asking questions about what had happened when Ellen Robb registered and what had happened right afterwards, whether she had any visitors.

"So then the motel manager recalled this man and—"

"Get a good look at him?" Mason asked.

"Apparently a hell of a good look," Drake said. "The fellow walked right past the light which shines out from the office, and the manager described the guy. The description fits Helman Ellis to a T. Moreover, after my man got to asking questions, the fellow remembered that he'd smoothed out this crumpled sheet of paper with the license number on it and had put it in the drawer of the desk. Then the next day he put in some timetables and some memos and he wondered if that crumpled piece of paper might not still be in there.

"So sure enough, he dug into the drawer and pulled out that crumpled piece of paper. There's one break in the case."

"What's that?" Mason asked.

"My man pretended that the incident didn't have any particular importance and managed to get possession of that crumpled piece of paper. We've checked the license number. It's the number of Helman Ellis' automobile."

"That little tramp!" Della Street said bitterly. "Double-crossing us like that!"

Mason said, "She swore up and down there was nothing between her and Ellis, that she hadn't seen him since before that final blowup at The Big Barn Tuesday night."

"I take it," Drake said dryly, "that leaves you behind the eight ball."

"Just as far behind the eight ball as you can get," Mason

said. "Now I *know* my client was lying and that puts me in the position of being an accomplice."

"Perry," Drake asked, "did you actually substitute guns?"

Mason said, "I don't need any rehearsal, Paul."

"What do you mean?"

"Hamilton Burger is going to pour the questions at me and I'll be busy answering them then. If you want to know what happened, listen to me on the witness stand."

"If you *did*," Drake said, "the murder must have been committed during the period between—"

Mason suddenly snapped his fingers. "Wait a minute, Paul. What's the time element in this thing?"

"What do you mean?" Drake asked.

Mason said, "Our office work sheets show the time that Ellen Robb left the office. Now then, I'll tell you this much, Paul. If a bullet was fired into the body of Nadine Ellis from the gun which Ellen Robb had with her when she was arrested, it had to be fired during the interval of time between the hour she left the office here, Wednesday morning, and the time she showed up at the Surf and Sea Motel. So let's check the time element there."

"What good will that do?" Drake asked. "You *know* she had the opportunity because she did it. There must have been sufficient time for the murder to have been committed because she *did* go to the yacht and she *did* fire the bullet from that gun—if the district attorney's theory is right and you switched guns on her—and I take it that the theory is right."

"Take any theory you want to," Mason said. "I'm not making any admissions—not yet."

"Well, I can give you the time she checked in at the motel," Drake said. "It was at eleven-fifty, Tuesday night."

Mason nodded to Della Street. "Let's get our work sheets, Della. Let's see what time she left the office."

Della Street opened the date book to the date, ran down the page of the date book and said, "She arrived here at nine-twenty on the morning of Wednesday the tenth and left at nine-forty-five.''

Mason said, "Mrs. Ellis was alive Wednesday morning. Her husband saw her early that morning.''

"She couldn't have committed the crime after seven on Wednesday evening,'' Drake said, "because we had a bodyguard on the job. She was virtually under surveillance. Moreover, she went to the motel in a taxicab Tuesday night. Wednesday morning she went out before the manager saw her. Presumably she went to the bus station, took a bus and then a cab to your office. She left your office, took a bus back to Costa Mesa and then a taxi to the motel.

"We've traced her on the journey back to Costa Mesa and there's no question of the time schedule there. The manager is certain she didn't leave the motel again Wednesday afternoon, and then our bodyguards were on the job.

"So she must have killed Mrs. Ellis on the yacht between 6:00 A.M. Wednesday when the evidence shows Mrs. Ellis left for the yacht, and the time she would have had to have taken a bus to get to your office Wednesday morning.''

"Provided she took a bus,'' Mason said. "She could have used taxicabs, and stopped by the yacht club long enough to have committed the murder and then gone to my office.''

Drake said, "Ten to one, Perry, that's exactly what she did, and Hamilton Burger is going to come up with the cab-drivers who will identify her.''

Mason was thoughtful. "You had men watching the unit of the motel. You were guarding against people who might have tried to hurt her, but she wasn't under surveillance.''

Drake shook his head. "There was only one door in that motel unit, Perry. My men were watching to see that no one went in who might intend to make trouble and, by the same sign, they can also be sure that no one went out.''

"Your men are thoroughly dependable?'' Mason asked.

"The best.''

"And they keep records?''

"Just like your own time records,'' Drake said.

"The men didn't leave for anything?"

"Not a thing," Drake said. "There were two men on the job. When one of them would go to report or powder his nose, the other man would be there waiting. You told me you wanted a one-hundred per cent job of bodyguarding and you got a one-hundred per cent job of bodyguarding."

"And when I went out there," Mason said. "I told you to dismiss the bodyguards."

"You told me to dismiss the bodyguards, but Mrs. Ellis was dead by that time—that was shortly before Ellen Robb was arrested."

A slow smile twitched at the corners of Paul Drake's mouth. "Perhaps," he said, "you can get Hamilton Burger's theory fouled up on the time element but . . ." He let his voice trail into silence, then shrugged his shoulders.

"Exactly," Mason said. "Your mind has run up against the fact that the proof is mathematical. The bullet was fired from that gun. If I gave her that gun, Paul, she fired the bullet from it after I gave it to her. And she simply had to have had time to fire the bullet, regardless of *when* she fired the bullet."

"But if Nadine Ellis was dead at the time the second bullet was fired," Drake said, "the crime is simply that of desecrating a corpse. That's only a misdemeanor. It may not be that."

"You're forgetting the implications," Mason said. "If she knew where the body was and if she went and fired a second bullet into it, it was because she had committed the murder and was taking advantage of this legal technicality she overheard me discuss over the telephone."

Mason looked at his wrist watch, sighed, and said, "Well, this is the end of a perfect day, Paul. We're going to have to leave for court in order to be there at eight o'clock. As long as I can find some way to cross-examine Ellis, I can stall off the fatal blow, but the minute I quit asking him questions Burger will call me as a witness and then I'm all washed up— and the worst of it is Judge Keyser knows exactly what the

179

score is and doesn't intend to let me stall. I've got to use all my ingenuity to prolong this case until I can figure out some way of keeping off that witness stand.''

Mason helped Della Street on with her coat, switched off the lights.

As they went out the door Paul Drake said, ''I know now how a fellow feels when they come to get him on the day of the execution and start leading him along the last mile to the gas chamber.''

''Nice feeling, isn't it?'' Della Street said.

Mason might not have heard them. His eyes thoughtful, he walked toward the elevators with the same steady rhythm that had marked his pacing of the office floor.

Chapter 14

Judge Keyser surveyed the crowded courtroom with stern eyes as he stood at the bench. Then he seated himself, and the bailiff said, "Be seated."

Hamilton Burger arose. "Your Honor," he said, "pursuant to the understanding and the demand of defense counsel, George Anclitas has here in this brief case the three weapons from his place of business.

"I wish to submit to the Court that one of these guns which have been produced is of some significant evidentiary value in the case, because it now appears that one of these guns fired the other bullet which was taken from the body of Nadine Ellis.

"If the Court please, since there is no jury here, I am going to state to the Court certain facts in connection with these guns.

"We have in evidence the gun which was found in the yacht, the *Cap's Eyes*. This gun was the one which was purchased by George Anclitas' partner and given to Helman Ellis by George Anclitas. We will call this the Ellis gun. It is Exhibit E in this case.

"We also have the revolver, Exhibit B, which was found in the possession of the defendant.

"Now, just in order to keep the records straight, I wish to state that during the recess the ballistics expert, Alexander Redfield, fired test bullets from the three guns which were in the possession of George Anclitas. This was done for the purpose of protecting our interests in the case. It is a well-known fact that when he is defending a client in a murder case Mr. Perry Mason can juggle guns around so that the

Court, the witnesses and the issues become confused. We don't want that to happen in this case.

"Now then I will state that, to the surprise of the prosecution, it turns out that one of these guns in the possession of George Anclitas *did* fire the bullet which was recovered from the body of Nadine Ellis and which bullet is in evidence as People's Exhibit C-1.

"Despite the fact the barrel has since been defaced, we are in a position to show that this is the same gun which was submitted to Maurice Halstead for test purposes, that it was in the possession of Mr. Perry Mason; that is, it was given to Maurice Halstead by Paul Drake, a detective employed by Perry Mason in this case.

"This gives us three weapons which are either involved in the case or which will be involved in the case. That leaves two more weapons which are not involved in any way in the case, and I now suggest that the Court make an order releasing George Anclitas from further attendance and releasing him from any obligation in response to a defense *subpoena duces tecum* to bring those guns into court.

"We have a total of three revolvers here, and I propose to see that those revolvers are kept separate and described in such a way that there can be no confusion. I certainly don't want to have any more weapons brought into the case. I am making this statement, not as evidence, but simply in order to apprise the Court of the situation and in connection with a motion asking the Court to release George Anclitas from further attendance and removing those two guns, which have nothing to do with the case, from the courtroom."

"Now, just a minute," Judge Keyser said. "The Court wants to know one thing. This gun which fired the bullet, Exhibit C-1, has a mark on the front sight where a nail file cut a groove in it?"

"Yes, Your Honor," Hamilton Burger said. "However, I will state that I am satisfied this could not have been the gun which was given to Ellis.

"I think there can be no question but that this witness was

182

the victim of an honest mistake when he stated that this mark had been made upon the front sight of the gun which was given to Helman Ellis. We have proof of that. Helman Ellis remembers the circumstances perfectly, and I expect to show by him exactly what did happen. I had announced that I was finished with the witness so that I could call Perry Mason to the stand, but since Mason refused to stipulate the entire testimony of the witness could go out, and since the witness is in court—having merely been withdrawn from the stand so George Anclitas could take the stand—I now wish to recall the witness, Ellis, to the stand.''

Judge Keyser looked meaningly at Perry Mason and said, ''In view of the fact that this is only a preliminary hearing, that the Court has called for a night session in order to clear up certain matters, the Court certainly doesn't intend to permit counsel for either side to consume time with any general fishing expeditions. The questions and answers will conform to the strict rules of evidence.

''Now, Mr. Burger, you may proceed. Mr. Ellis, return to the stand, please.''

Hamilton Burger, glancing at the clock, looking back at the spectators, noticing the array of newspaper reporters in the front row, smiled triumphantly and said, ''Mr. Ellis, do you recall the circumstances under which Mr. Anclitas gave you a revolver?''

''Very clearly.''

''Will you state to the Court what those circumstances were?''

''Mr. Anclitas and his partner, W. W. Marcus, had made a bet of some kind about a revolver. I didn't know exactly what the bet was but I did see Slim Marcus—I beg the Court's pardon, I mean W. W. Marcus—pay fifty dollars to George Anclitas and at that time Mr. Anclitas was holding a gun in his hand. I admired the gun and said that I was going to get one for the purpose of protection and at that time Slim—that is, Mr. Marcus—reached under the counter or bar and pulled out a gun which was exactly similar and said something to

183

the effect that, 'We have too many guns. We might as well give him one' and at that time George Anclitas presented me with the gun which Mr. Marcus had handed to me.

"That, however, was not the gun which Mr. Anclitas had been holding in his hand when he returned from the barber-shop and beauty parlor where he and his partner had been making a bet."

Hamilton Burger nodded and smiled at the Court. "That explains it, I think, Your Honor," he said. "I have no further questions."

"Do you have some cross-examination?" Judge Keyser asked Perry Mason.

"Yes, Your Honor."

"Please be advised that under the circumstances the Court will try to give you all reasonable latitude in cross-examination but will not countenance any tactics to gain time or any questions which may be asked for the purpose of delay," Judge Keyser said. "You may proceed with the cross-examination."

"Are you in love with the defendant in this case?" Mason asked.

"No, sir."

"Were you at any time in love with her?"

"Objected to as not proper cross-examination," Hamilton Burger said.

"Overruled," Judge Keyser announced.

"I think I was at one time. At least I was infatuated with her."

"Is it true that your wife discovered this infatuation?" Mason asked.

"Objected to as not proper cross-examination," Hamilton Burger said.

Mason said, "If the Court please, the prosecution's own witnesses have stated that there was a scene between the defendant and Nadine Ellis. I am entitled to cross-examine this witness on it."

"If the Court please," Hamilton Burger said, "of course

we showed that altercation, and if counsel had wanted to cross-examine *that* witness on *that* altercation he had that right, but *this* witness has given no such testimony and therefore *this* is not proper cross-examination.''

''Except insofar as it may go to show bias of the witness,'' Judge Keyser said, hesitating perceptibly in an attempt to be scrupulously fair.

''What has happened in the past doesn't show the bias of the witness,'' Hamilton Burger said. ''The fact that his wife became jealous doesn't show the witness' bias. The question is, what is in the mind of the witness at the present time? What is his relation toward the defendant? What are his thoughts? What are his feelings? His bias? His prejudice? Or his lack of bias or prejudice?''

''And I submit, if the Court please,'' Mason said, ''that the only proper way to show that is not by asking the witness how he feels but by showing the relationship which has existed between the parties.''

''I think that is correct,'' Judge Keyser said, ''but I will not permit a report of an account of an altercation between the decedent and the defendant by way of cross-examination at this time and of this witness.''

''I'll reframe the question,'' Mason said.

Mason turned to the witness. ''At a time when your wife and the defendant had an altercation over you, and accusations were made by your wife, were you present and did you take any part in the altercation?''

''Same objection,'' Hamilton Burger said.

''This question is permissible,'' Judge Keyser said.

''I make the further objection that it assumes a fact not in evidence.''

''But it is in evidence,'' Judge Keyser said, ''not by this witness but by your own witnesses. The objection is overruled. Answer the question.''

''I took no part,'' Ellis said.

''Did you see the defendant on the eighth of this month?''

''Yes, sir.''

"At The Big Barn where she was working?"

"Yes, sir."

"Were you present when she was discharged on Tuesday, the ninth?"

"No, sir."

"Did you see her that same night after she had been discharged?"

"I saw her before she was discharged."

"That isn't the question. Did you see her afterwards?"

"I . . . I don't remember."

"Let's see if we can refresh your memory," Mason said. "The defendant went to the Surf and Sea Motel in Costa Mesa. Did you go there?"

"Yes, that's right. I did."

"And saw her there?"

"Very briefly."

"When did you next see her?"

"I don't remember. I think . . . I don't think I saw her after that until she had been arrested."

"You don't remember?"

"I can't say positively, no, sir."

"This was a girl with whom you had been infatuated and yet you can't remember whether you saw her or not?"

"Sure I saw her but it was after she had been arrested. I can't remember. I saw her so many times that it was difficult to keep them straight."

"You remember seeing her at the Surf and Sea Motel?"

"Yes, sir."

"That was on the night of Tuesday, the ninth of this month?"

"Yes, sir."

"How long did you see her on that occasion?"

"About ten or fifteen minutes."

"Where did you go after you left the defendant that night?"

"Objected to as incompetent, irrelevant and not proper cross-examination," Hamilton Burger said. "This witness is not on trial."

"I have a right to test his recollection," Mason said.

"You're trying to test his recollection in regard to matters which have absolutely nothing to do with the case," Hamilton Burger said. "If you start following every move made by this witness over the period of time from Tuesday, the ninth, until the body of his wife was discovered, you'll have this court sitting here all night inquiring into matters which have absolutely nothing to do with the case."

"The objection is sustained," Judge Keyser said.

"Did your wife tell you that she had been advised by her attorney that in case two bullets were fired into a body by two persons acting independently that only the person firing the bullet which actually resulted in death was guilty of murder?" Mason asked.

"Objected to as incompetent, irrelevant and immaterial, calling for hearsay, not proper cross-examination," Hamilton Burger said.

"Sustained," Judge Keyser snapped.

"You were at The Big Barn on the night of Tuesday, the ninth?"

"Yes."

"All right," Mason said, "I'm going to put it to you directly. Didn't you at that time take possession of one of the guns in The Big Barn? Now remember, you're under oath."

"What do you mean by 'take possession'?"

"I'm asking you," Mason said, "if you didn't arrange with Sadie Bradford to pick up one of the guns and turn it over to you."

"Just a moment, Your Honor," Hamilton Burger said. "This is getting far afield. This is not proper cross-examination. It is—"

Judge Keyser, leaning forward looking at the witness's face, said suddenly, "I think it is. The Court wants an answer to that question. Did you or did you not, Mr. Ellis?"

The witness shifted his position once more, moistened his lips with the tip of his tongue, said finally, "Yes, I did."

"And," Mason said, "didn't you kill your wife with that

187

gun? Then didn't you arrange with Sadie Bradford to put that gun in the baggage of this defendant while the defendant was in the powder room? Thereafter didn't the defendant tell you that she had consulted me? Didn't you therefore on Wednesday morning examine the gun which was in the defendant's possession and find that it was not the gun that you had planted? Didn't you thereupon surreptitiously remove the gun the defendant had in her baggage on Wednesday, go down to your yacht and fire another bullet from that gun into the dead body of your wife? Then didn't you surreptitiously return that gun to the defendant's bag? Didn't you do all of this without her knowledge before bodyguards had been employed to protect the defendant, all the time assuring her of your great love and devotion and telling her that you would arrange to marry her as soon as the necessary arrangements could be made, but swearing her to complete and utter secrecy?''

"Your Honor, Your Honor,'' Hamilton Burger shouted, "this is the height of absurdity! This is the most fantastic, preposterous idea ever promulgated by counsel in an attempt to save his own skin! It is—''

"It is,'' Judge Keyser interrupted in low, level tones, "a question which certainly tends to show the bias of the witness. Under the circumstances I am going to permit it. The witness will answer the question.''

White to the lips, Helman Ellis said, "I did not.''

There was a sudden commotion in the rear of the courtroom.

The young woman who came marching determinedly forward said, "I see it all now. That's *exactly* what he did! He used me as a cat's-paw. I want to surrender and turn state's evidence.''

The bailiff started to pound for silence. One of the officers jumped up to grab the woman, but Judge Keyser restrained the officer with his hand, said, "Silence,'' to the bailiff, turned to the woman and said, "Who are you?''

"I'm Sadie Bradford, the hat-check girl,'' she said. "I

realize now exactly what he did. He used me for an accomplice.''

Judge Keyser looked at Perry Mason. The puzzled perplexity in his eyes slowly changed to grudging admiration. ''I think,'' he said, ''the Court will, of its own motion, continue this matter until tomorrow morning at ten o'clock, and I suggest that the district attorney endeavor to unscramble this situation before court convenes tomorrow.''

''I insist upon calling Perry Mason as a witness tonight, and in connection with this preliminary examination,'' Hamilton Burger shouted.

Judge Keyser smiled at him. ''I think, Mr. District Attorney, that on sober second thought you will be glad that you didn't call Mr. Mason. Court has adjourned.''

Judge Keyser got up and left the bench.

Mason continued to stand. His facial expression gave no indication of his inner thoughts.

Newspaper reporters, swarming through the gate in the mahogany rail, pelted him with questions. Photographers exploded flash bulbs.

''No comment,'' Mason said. ''I will reserve any statement until after tomorrow morning at ten o'clock.''

Chapter 15

A weary Hamilton Burger arose, tried to ignore the crowded courtroom and addressed himself to Judge Keyser.

"If the Court please," he said, "the prosecution moves for the dismissal of the case against Ellen Robb, and in making that motion the prosecution feels it only fair to state to the Court that Helman Ellis has given a signed confession, that Helman Ellis was to some extent infatuated with Ellen Robb. He was also, however, having an affair with Sadie Bradford, the young woman who doubled as a hat-check girl and as attendant in the ladies' powder room. Ellis is an opportunist, and he was no longer interested in his wife.

"It is true that George Anclitas gave Helman Ellis a gun. This gun was kept in Ellis' house. According to Helman Ellis' confession, he secured possession of one of the other guns which was kept behind the bar in The Big Barn for protection against holdups. On Tuesday evening Helman Ellis shot his wife with this gun while they were aboard his yacht, the *Cap's Eyes*. In order to make it appear that his wife had been defending herself against an assailant, he took the gun which George Anclitas had given him and, after he had murdered his wife, fired a shot into the woodwork near the cabin door, then cocked the gun again and left the cocked and loaded revolver by the dead body of his wife, near her right hand.

"Helman Ellis then returned to The Big Barn, saw the defendant, and also saw his friend, Sadie Bradford. He persuaded Sadie Bradford to plant the gun with which the murder had been committed in the baggage of Ellen Robb, hoping that it would remain there until it was discovered by the police. Sadie Bradford had no knowledge of the murder. Ellis persuaded her to plant the gun because he said he wanted to have Ellen Robb discharged so he could terminate an affair with her.

"Later on, through his friend Sadie Bradford, Ellis learned of the altercation which had resulted in the discharge of Ellen Robb and learned that Ellen Robb had telephoned the Surf and Sea Motel for a reservation, stating that she intended to go there for the night. Helman Ellis immediately drove to the motel, waited for Ellen to arrive, and then under the guise of his great affection for her and his desire to help her, first convinced himself that the gun had indeed been planted in Ellen's baggage and then persuaded Ellen that she must under no circumstances admit that she had seen him that evening at the motel or that there was anything between them.

"Thereafter, according to his confession which we now have reason to accept at its face value, Helman Ellis left the motel, drove directly to the yacht club, loosened the yacht from its mooring, drifted with the tide until he was able to start the motors without anyone at the yacht club knowing the boat had been cast loose. He then took the boat to Catalina Island and caught the morning plane back to the mainland.

"Knowing that Ellen Robb planned to call on Perry Mason, he made it a point to see her after she had left Mason's office. He walked with her to the place where she was to take the bus to Costa Mesa and got her to describe in detail her visit to Perry Mason's office.

"When Ellen Robb had told him that Mason had told her to keep the gun in her possession and had done nothing about it, Ellis became suspicious and got Ellen to show him the gun which she was then carrying in her purse.

"We now come to the interesting part of Helman Ellis' confession which was designed to completely baffle the investigators. The gun which George Anclitas had given to Helman Ellis was not the gun that had the scratch on the front sight. But the gun with which the murder had been

191

committed, and which had been planted in the bag of Ellen Robb, did have that scratch on the front sight. Ellis had a shrewd suspicion that perhaps Mason in an attempt to protect his client had substituted guns, giving her an entirely different gun, and when he inspected the gun which Ellen Robb showed him, he was convinced that this was the case because that gun did not have a scratch on the front sight.

"Ellis persuaded Ellen Robb that it would be dangerous for her to carry the gun which was then in her purse, on the bus. He said that she might be apprehended for carrying a concealed weapon. He said that Mr. Mason had undoubtedly given her the right advice and that she should return the gun to the bag where she had found it, but that it would be better if *she* did not carry that gun in her purse since she had no permit. He therefore volunteered to take possession of the gun and return it to her possession later on in the day so that she could then put it back in the bag where she had found it. But he persuaded her that under no circumstances must she tell anyone of his intercession in the matter or of his interest.

"He then explained to Ellen Robb that he had some business matters to attend to, left her at the bus station, drove at once to an air field where he rented a plane, since he has a flier's license, and flew to Catalina Island. There he again sought out the yacht, unlocked the cabin door, fired a shot from this second gun into the dead body of his wife, locked the cabin door of the yacht, sailed it around to the other side of the island, tied it up to a convenient rock, pointed the yacht out to sea, locked the steering gear in position, started the motor, then untied the doubled rope and let the yacht head out to sea. He then returned to the place where he had left his rented airplane, flew back to Los Angeles, went to the office of Perry Mason and persuaded Perry Mason that Ellen Robb was in danger of attack from Nadine Ellis— knowing that Mason would in all probability hire bodyguards to protect his client.

"Thereafter Ellis, according to his confession, drove to the Surf and Sea Motel, entering the place through a driveway back of the alley where he would not be noticed. He explained to Ellen Robb that he had done her a great favor in bringing the gun back to her but that she must never mention his connection with the matter. He swore his undying love and affection for her and promised her that they would be married when he could arrange with his wife to get a divorce.

"Again, according to the confession of Ellis, which apparently is true, he did not know about the proscribed area for small boats off Catalina Island. He thought that his yacht would sail out into the ocean until the fuel tanks were exhausted, that then it would probably be capsized during some storm, and sink. He knew that the boat was hardly seaworthy. If, however, anything happened and the boat *was* discovered, he knew that the body of his wife would contain a bullet fired from a gun which was in the possession of Ellen Robb. And he felt certain that by having arranged the crime as he did, he could give himself a perfect alibi.

"Now then, if the Court please, that is the gist of the confession of Helman Ellis. I feel it my duty as an officer of the court to disclose that confession at this time in connection with a motion to dismiss the case against Ellen Robb. I feel that she has been victimized and I wish to make this statement so that the facts can be made public."

Judge Keyser regarded Hamilton Burger thoughtfully. Then his eyes shifted to Perry Mason. "The Court still doesn't understand how it happened that the gun which was originally placed in the defendant's baggage was returned to the possession of George Anclitas."

Hamilton Burger said wearily, "It seems that Sadie Bradford, while working as attendant in the women's powder room, found this gun on the floor of the powder room at a time when she had momentarily stepped to the door to talk with Helman Ellis. She feels certain that Helman Ellis had placed the gun on the floor, and that when she opened the powder-room door, she had kicked the gun into position under one of the washbowls. She knows that the gun was not there when she stepped to the door. There was no one in the powder room at the time. When she returned from her conversation with Mr. Ellis, the gun was lying there under the washbowl. She therefore picked it up and returned it to its place under the bar, feeling that in so doing she was following the wishes of Helman Ellis.

"The perplexing point is that Helman Ellis, while confessing the murder, still insists that he had nothing to do with returning that gun to the washroom. However, under the circumstances and in view of the fact that the powder room is ventilated entirely by fans and has no windows, that there is no door to the powder room except the one door where the witness, Sadie Bradford, was standing, it would seem that for some reason which I confess I can't understand at the time, Helman Ellis is continuing to lie about returning that gun—and for the life of me," Hamilton Burger blurted, "I can't see why he would lie about it unless it was in an attempt to involve Perry Mason as counsel for the defense.

"It now appears that Perry Mason acted unconventionally but not illegally. Having been advised that a gun had been planted in a suitcase in the defendant's possession, he had test bullets fired from that gun and gave them to a ballistics expert for checking. In doing this he was quite probably within his rights."

"I still don't see how the Crowder gun could have been placed in the purse of Ellen Robb unless it was done by her counsel."

"May I address the Court, Your Honor?" Mason asked.

"Certainly, Mr. Mason."

"When my client came to my office and stated that someone had planted a gun in her suitcase, I desired an opportunity to examine that gun," Mason said. "I felt that I was well within my rights in so doing, particularly in view of the fact that there was no indication that any crime had been committed at that time. I substituted a gun from my office in such a way that the defendant would not know there had been any substitution of guns.

194

"I feel that any attorney who is confident that someone has attempted to involve his client by planting stolen property in her possession is entitled to take such steps to see to it that in any search of his client's possessions designed to produce that stolen property, the property recovered may not necessarily be the property which was deliberately planted in the possession of the client."

"So far so good," Judge Keyser said. "The Court is inclined to agree with you there, although it is certainly an unconventional procedure. The proper procedure would have been to report to the police."

"That is a matter of expediency and depends upon the circumstances," Perry Mason said.

"However, as to all the rest of this," Judge Keyser said, "with all of this manipulation of weapons and the fact that it appears a murder had been committed with the weapon which apparently had been planted in the baggage of your client, Mr. Mason, how do you account for subsequent events?"

"I don't think *I* have to account for them," Mason said. "I have exonerated my client, I have exposed a murderer. If my methods were unconventional, they were at least effective."

Judge Keyser smiled.

Hamilton Burger, his face somewhat red, said, "If there was any possible opportunity for Perry Mason to have been in any way connected with the return of that weapon to the powder room in The Big Barn, I would feel differently about it. As it is, I have only the word of a confessed murderer and his accomplice as to what happened and I am satisfied that regardless of the truth of what has been told me, the situation as disclosed by Sadie Bradford, who has now become a state's witness, is such that it would have been impossible for Perry Mason to have placed that gun where it was found. I feel Helman Ellis entertains a bitter hatred for Perry Mason because of the way Mason interfered with his well-laid plans for murdering his wife. In some way Ellis secured possession

195

of that gun and returned it to the women's powder room, hoping to involve Mr. Mason.

"Quite obviously, Mr. Mason, who must have acted very unconventionally if not illegally, is not going to betray the confidences of his client. Since my own witnesses say Mr. Ellis must have had that gun in his possession and returned it to the washroom, and since the only witness against Perry Mason is now a self-confessed murderer with a vindictive hatred of counsel, and since it appears counsel's client is innocent, I am convinced that whatever happened it would be impossible to proceed against Perry Mason. If I did so, moreover, I would be questioning the integrity of one of the prosecution's own witnesses and weakening my case against Helman Ellis, who, incidentally, has now repudiated his confession and insists that it was obtained by coercion and promises of immunity."

Perry Mason said, "If the prosecutor is satisfied that it was impossible for *me* to have returned that gun, I certainly am not one to contradict him."

Judge Keyser gave the matter long and earnest thought, then finally shook his head. "This is a situation," he said, "which completely baffles the Court. However, it is now quite apparent that in view of the circumstances as disclosed by the prosecutor, whatever counsel did to protect his client who was completely innocent of any wrongdoing, resulted not only in the acquittal of an innocent person but the detection and arrest of the guilty person.

"Under those circumstances it seems that there is nothing for the Court to do except . . . dismiss the case against Ellen Robb, release her from custody, and take a recess."

Judge Keyser arose from the bench, started toward his chambers, paused, glanced thoughtfully at Perry Mason, shook his head and then hurried on into chambers.

Hamilton Burger, surrounded by reporters anxious to learn the details of Ellis' confession, had no chance to exchange any comments with Perry Mason, and Perry Mason, winking at Della Street, took advantage of the confusion to hurry from the courtroom.

"How in the world did you know?" Della Street asked him as they descended in the elevator.

"Because," Mason said, "it was the only thing that could have happened. From the time Ellen Robb got that gun from me she didn't have time to find the yacht, fire the bullet into the body of Nadine Ellis and return to the Surf and Sea Motel. Remember that Drake traced her movements from the bus depot to the motel.

"The only thing that *could* have happened was that the boat with the body of Nadine Ellis must have been taken to sea in two installments. First, a night cruise to some isolated cove in Catalina; then, in the second stage, being pointed out to sea and left to run out of fuel. The only place I could think of where the yacht could have made such a two-stage cruise was by stopping at Catalina and, quite obviously, Ellen Robb had no opportunity to get to Catalina on at least two different occasions.

"Moreover, once I stopped to think of it, I realized that the gun which was found in the cabin with Nadine Ellis must have been planted there after Mrs. Ellis had been killed. One shot had been fired from that gun, and the gun, fully cocked, was lying on the cabin floor near her hand.

"When a person tries to do accurate shooting with a double-action gun, he quite frequently pulls back the hammer so as to work the mechanism with a simple pull of the trigger, but when one is trying for rapid shots at close range, there is no time to cock the gun manually. Almost invariably, under such circumstances, a person uses the double-action mechanism and in so doing it would be impossible for the gun to have been fully cocked after the first shot had been fired. Therefore I began to suspect the gun had been a plant and if it had been planted, then the bullet fired into the woodwork of the cabin was designed to throw us off the trail.

"After that it was simple, once I realized that the bullet from the Anclitas gun must have been fired first. That meant that Mrs. Ellis must have been dead when I handed Ellen Robb the other gun. Then the yacht must have started to Catalina Island before Ellen Robb came to my office. This meant Helman Ellis must have been lying about that whole conversation he claimed he had with his wife on Wednesday morning. For one thing, the Ellises had only one car, and the evidence that Helman drove it to Ellen's motel Tuesday night precluded the possibility that Mrs. Ellis had driven it to Phoenix Tuesday evening. Once I started on that chain of reasoning, I knew what *must* have happened.''

''But how did you know the bullet from the Anclitas gun was the *first* bullet?''

''Because I marked the barrel with an etching tool before it left our possession, and the bullet recovered from the body of Mrs. Ellis didn't show those marks which would have been on it if it had been fired after I marked the barrel with the etching tool.''

''Well,'' Della Street said, ''you certainly had your back to the wall that time. Is this going to teach you not to take chances on behalf of your clients in the future?''

Mason grinned and shook his head. ''It's simply going to teach me to practice the art of concentration,'' he said. ''I never thought as fast or as hard in my life as I did from the time court adjourned yesterday afternoon until I threw the crucial question at Helman Ellis in cross-examination last night.

''When I left that courtroom, I felt as though I had been put through a wringer.''

Della Street looked up at him with admiration in her eyes. ''Yet during all of that time,'' she said, ''you never wavered in your loyalty to your client, despite the fact that you were virtually certain she had lied to you.''

Mason heaved a sigh. ''Della,'' he said, ''whenever I waver in my loyalty to a client, do me a favor. Just close up the office, get some paint remover and erase the words ATTORNEY AT LAW from the door of the reception room.''

About the Author

Erle Stanley Gardner is the king of American mystery fiction. A criminal lawyer, he filled his mystery masterpieces with intricate, fascinating, ever-twisting plots. Challenging, clever, and full of surprises, these are whodunits in the best tradition. During his lifetime, Erle Stanley Gardner wrote 146 books, 85 of which feature Perry Mason.

SHREWD and SUSPENSEFUL...
MYSTICAL and MYSTERIOUS

THE PERRY MASON MYSTERIES
by
ERLE STANLEY
GARDNER